Adventurous Me

Me, You, and Us Series: Book 1

by

Deanndra Hall

Adventurous Me
Me, You, and Us Series: Book 1

ISBN-13: 978-0615958910
ISBN-10: 0615958915
Print Edition

Celtic Muse Publishing, LLC
P.O. Box 3722
Paducah, KY 42002-3722

This book is a work of fiction.

Names of characters, places, and events are the construction of the author, except those locations that are well-known and of general knowledge, and all are used fictitiously. Any resemblance to persons living or dead is coincidental, and great care was taken to design places, locations, or businesses that fit into the regional landscape without actual identification; as such, resemblance to actual places, locations, or businesses is coincidental. Any mention of a branded item, artistic work, or well-known business establishment, is used for authenticity in the work of fiction and was chosen by the author because of personal preference, its high quality, or the authenticity it lends to the work of fiction; the author has received no remuneration, either monetary or in-kind, for use of said product names, artistic work, or business establishments, and mention is not intended as advertising, nor does it constitute an endorsement. The author is solely responsible for content.

Cover design by Novel Graphic Designs, used by permission of the artist
Formatting by BB eBooks

Disclaimer:

Material in this work of fiction is of a graphic sexual nature and is not intended for audiences under 18 years of age.

More titles from this author:

Love Under Construction Series

The Groundbreaking **(Free Introductory Volume)**

The Groundbreaking is a preview of the main characters contained in all of the Love Under Construction Series books. Not intended as a work of erotic fiction, it is simply a way for the reader to get to know and love each character by discovering their backgrounds. Contains graphic situations that are unsuitable for readers under 18 years old.

Laying a Foundation **(Book 1)**

Sometimes death robs us of the life we thought we'd have; sometimes a relationship that just won't die can be almost as bad. And sometimes the universe aligns to take care of everything. When you've spent years alone, regardless the circumstances, getting back out there can be hard. But when you've finally opened up to love and it looks like you might lose it all, can love be enough to see you through?

Tearing Down Walls **(Book 2)**

Secrets – they can do more damage than the truth. Secrets have kept two people from realizing their full potential, but even worse, have kept them from forming lasting relationships and finding the love and acceptance they both desperately need. Can they finally let go of those secrets in time to find love – and maybe even to stay alive?

Renovating a Heart **(Book 3)**

Can a person's past really be so bad that they can never recover from it? Sometimes it seems that way. One man hides the truth of a horrific loss in his teen years; one woman hides the truth of a broken, scarred life that took a wrong turn in her teens. Can they be honest with each other, or even with themselves, about their feelings? And will they be able to go that distance before one of them is lost forever?

Planning an Addition **(Book 4)**

When you think you're set for life and that life gets yanked out from under you, starting over is hard. One woman who's starting over finds herself in love with two men who've started over too, and she's forced to choose. Or is she? And when one of them is threatened by their past, everyone has choices to make. Can they make the right ones in time to save a life?

The Harper's Cove Series

Beginning with the flagship volume, Karen and Brett at 326 Harper's Cove, find out exactly what the neighbors of Harper's Cove are up to when they go inside and close their doors. According the Gloria, the drunken busy-body of the cove, they're all up to something perverse, and she's determined to find out their secrets. As she sneaks, peeks, pokes, and prods, her long-suffering husband, Russell, begs her to leave all of their nice neighbors alone. But could Gloria be right?

The Harper's Cove series books are fast, fun, nasty little reads priced just right to provide a quick, naughty romp. See if each of the couples of Harper's Cove shock you just enough to find out what the neighbors at the next address will do!

Karen and Brett at 326 Harper's Cove

Gloria wants more than anything to be invited to one of Karen and Brett Reynolds' parties, and she's very vocal about it. Karen and Brett, however, know full well that if Gloria were ever invited to one of their parties, she would be in a hurry to leave, and in an even bigger hurry to let everyone know they're the scourge of the neighborhood. Every Saturday night, Karen and Brett keep their secrets – all twelve of them.

Donna and Connor at 228 Harper's Cove

Those nice people at 228, the Millicans? They're religious counselors, trying to help lovely couples who are having marital problems. Problem is, they're not counseling;

training, maybe, but not counseling. But no matter what Donna says, Gloria still thinks the truck that delivered large crates to the Millicans' house in the wee hours of the morning two weeks after they'd moved in was pretty suspicious. Donna says it was exercise equipment that the moving company had lost, but Gloria's not so sure. Could it be that they're not as they appear?

Becca and Greg at 314 Harper's Cove

Even though they're quiet and stay to themselves, Becca and Greg Henderson seem pretty nice and average. They don't go out much or have many people over, except for that one couple who are probably relatives. But when that half-sister of Becca's moves in, it all seems a little fishy; she gets around pretty well for a person recovering from cancer. And where was Becca going all decked out in that weird outfit? The Henderson are tight-lipped, but Gloria hopes she can eventually get to the bottom of things. If she does, she'll get the biggest surprise of her life.

And we're just getting started!

A word from the author . . .

I don't really know where this novel came from.

One day the title just came to me. I'm not sure why. I wasn't looking for anything else to write – god knows I've got enough stuff on deck. But the title intrigued me, so I set out to write whatever the book was supposed to be.

And just when I thought it was a lost cause, Trish started to speak and everything fell into place. I met Sheila, and Dave, and Steffen, and then Clint, and Trish told me all about them through her eyes. I didn't quite know what I thought about it. But I found out pretty quick what my betas thought about it.

They loved it.

And so I offer it to you, a sweet little read full of sass and pain and passion and over-the-top, hardcore sex. And love – don't forget love. It's what makes the world go 'round, you know!

Love and happy reading,
Deanndra

Visit my website and blog at: www.deanndrahall.com

Connect with me on Substance B:
substance-b.com/DeanndraHall.html

Contact me at: DeanndraHall@gmail.com

Join me on Facebook at: facebook.com/deanndra.hall

Catch me on Twitter at: twitter.com/DeanndraHall

Write to me at: P.O. Box 3722, Paducah, KY 42002-3722

Support your Indie authors!

Independent (Indie) authors are not a new phenomenon, but they are a hard-working one. As Indie authors, we write our books, have trouble finding anyone to beta read them for us, seldom have money to hire an editor, struggle with our cover art, find it nearly impossible to get a reviewer to even glance at our books, and do all of our own publicity, promotion, and marketing. This is not something that we do until we find someone to offer us a contract – this is a conscious decision we've made to do for ourselves that which we'd have to do regardless (especially promotion, which publishers rarely do anyway). We do it so big publishing doesn't take our money and give us nothing in return. We do it because we do not want to give up rights to something on which we've worked so hard. And we do it because we want to offer you a convenient, quality product for an excellent price.

Indie authors try to bring their readers something fresh, fun, and different. Please help your Indie authors:

- Buy our books! That makes it possible for us to continue to produce them;
- If you like them, please go back to the retailer from which you bought them and review them for us. That helps us more than you could know;

- If you like them, please tell your friends, relatives, nail tech, lawn care guy, anyone you can find, about our books. Recommend them, please;
- If you're in a book circle, always contact an Indie author to see if you can get free or discounted books to use in your circle. Many would love to help you out;
- If you see our books being pirated, please let us know. We worked weekends, holidays, and through vacations (if we even get one) to put these books out, so please report it if you see them being stolen.

More than anything else, we hope you enjoy our books and, if you do, please contact us in whatever manner we've provided as it suits you. Visit our blogs and websites, friend our Facebook sites, and follow us on Twitter. We'd love to get to know you!

Chapter 1

"Goddamn it, Trish!" Ron ducks as I hurl another object. I'm not even sure what it was. It doesn't matter.

"Boring, huh? Tiresome, huh? Predictable, huh? Didn't predict this, did you, rat bastard?" I hurl an empty beer bottle at him. It misses his head by a fraction of an inch and crashes into the wall. I'm going to have a helluva mess to clean up, but right this minute, I don't care.

"Nuts! That's it, completely nuts! Trish, STOP IT!" He ducks again when I throw the crystal vase his parents gave us for our first anniversary.

Almost thirty years. That's what I've given this sad son of a bitch – almost thirty years. Wasted. No kids. Moved far away from my family.

And now I'm boring? Tiresome? Predictable?

Well, we'll just see about that!

"Yeah," I snarl into the phone. I know it's Sheila, but I still don't want to talk to anyone.

"Trish, what's wrong?" She's too damn good. I can't hide anything from her.

"Ron's leaving me."

"What? WHAT? Are you kidding? What the hell?"

"I wouldn't kid about a thing like that. Says I'm boring, predictable, tiresome. Can you believe that shit?" I'm still sweeping up glass. I sure threw a bunch of stuff. This is not a complaint; it's an observation. If I could've laid my hands on more stuff to throw, I would've.

"What are you going to do?" I know she's trying to be practical here, but I'm in no mood.

"I'm going to go get myself a drink, seeing as how I broke every bottle of beer in the house."

"Over his head?" I hear her giggle.

"No. I'm a lousy shot. But I wish." I straighten up and drop the broom and dustpan right where I'm standing. "I need something with vodka in it. Right now. You up for it?"

"Doesn't matter if I am or not. You're going to need a keeper tonight, so I guess that'll be me."

"You're gonna be *my* keeper? Good luck," I tell her. "You're gonna need it."

"You girls looking for anything in particular?" the guy who walks up to us asks. I look up at him through the vodka's haze. Good looking enough.

Sheila doesn't miss a beat. "No."

"Hey, I'll speak for myself!" I slur. "Yeah, I'm looking for adventure! Got any?"

"I'm sure we can come up with something!" he laughs and turns to the bartender. "Bring her another cosmo, wouldja?" Then he turns back to me. "My name's Jeff. What's yours?"

"Um," I say, not knowing if I should give him my real name; then I decide, what the hell? "Trish. I'm Trish. This one over here," I say, pointing at Sheila, "is Party Pooper." Somehow, everything I say is extremely funny.

"Well, Trish, I'm glad to meet you. And you too, PP," he laughs. "Want to go somewhere else, since you're feeling adventurous?"

"Sure! What've you got in mind?" I think I'm about to get laid, but it's been almost thirty years since I've dated, so I'm not really sure.

"Well, let's see, I have more vodka at my house, and a big flat-screen, and a big bed, and . . ."

Yep. I'm getting laid.

"Hell yeah! Let's go!" I try to get up off the stool and I almost crash into the man sitting on my other side. "Oh, shit, I'm sorry!"

He turns and says, "That's okay," but before he gets a chance to say another word, I get a look at him. A good look. He's got to be at least sixty, but he's the most gorgeous thing I've ever seen. White hair, white mustache and goatee, and luminous blue eyes with cute laugh crinkles around them. And he's wrapped in leather. One fine package. He's been sitting there most of the evening and I didn't even notice him. "You okay?" he asks me in a voice like melted caramel while he eyes Jeff.

"Yeah, yeah, I'm fine," I stammer. Suddenly I'm having trouble talking even though a minute and a half ago I was the funniest, most articulate woman in the world. I try to get up again – same result.

"Whoa! I think you'd better sit down until the room stops moving. Don't you think so, Jeff?" the man asks, and Jeff kind of shrinks.

"Hey, Trish, another time maybe?" Before I can answer, he's gone.

"Wait a minute! You ran off my piece of ass." I'm getting kind of pissed now.

Guy On Stool laughs. "You don't need that. Looks like you need a keeper!"

"Yeah, that's what old Party Pooper over there said." I point at Sheila. She's so disgusted with me that she's found someone else to talk to and she's ignoring me.

"Smart friend. Just sit here and keep me company. If you want." He sticks out his right hand. "Name's Dave. You're Trish?"

"Yeah, how did you . . . oh, right, Jeff." I shake my head and he laughs again, but I take his hand and shake it. He's got a nice grip, and his hands are strong but smooth.

"So I heard you say you're out looking for a little adventure. Is that right?" He picks up his on-the-rocks glass and puts it to his lips. Looking at his hands makes something inside me kind of vibrate in a funny way.

"Yeah. My rat bastard soon-to-be-ex says I'm boring and tedious, or something like that." I can't remember exactly what Ron said and, at this particular moment, I really don't care. "So I thought I'd show him."

"You do realize that trying to prove something to someone is a lousy reason to do something, don't you?" His gaze is serious.

I can feel my face burning. "Yes. I do. But I think that, in some ways, he might be right." I suddenly realize it's very embarrassing to say something like that to a total stranger, but there's a way about this guy that makes me trust him and want to talk to him.

He points at me. "Let me ask you something: When was the last time he took you on an adventure?" Dave then takes another sip of his drink while I ponder, and he's looking at me from under those beautiful dark lashes.

"Um, what do you mean?"

"Let's see . . . the last time he took you to do something that was potentially dangerous, like white-water rafting or rappelling? Or skydiving?" I shake my head. "Or when he took you on a discovery trip, like to an archaeological site, or a tour of an underground cavern, or to watch a colony of bats flying out of their cave as they're leaving for their evening feeding?" I shake my head again. "Where's the most adventurous place he ever had sex with you?"

I think for a minute. "Um, the living room?"

"Oh my god." Dave takes another swig and grins. "And he called *you* boring and tedious? He's got a lot of nerve." He shakes his head. "So what kind of adventure did you have in mind?"

I shrug. "I don't know. Obviously something I've never done before, or it wouldn't be an adventure, right?"

"And what haven't you done?"

"Most everything." Now I'm kind of ashamed. Maybe I really *am* boring.

"What size do you wear?"

"Huh?" That's a weird question for him to ask me.

"What size? Clothes? Shoes? What size do you wear?" He's looking me in the eye – he's dead serious about whatever it is that he's thinking.

"Um, a ten or a twelve? Shoes, a seven and a half."

"Want an adventure?" His eyes sparkle and those smile crinkles go into action.

"Maaaaayyybeeeeeee . . ."

"Well, if you do, just come by this address tomorrow night. I'll find you something to wear in the meantime. When you get there, just tell the doorman that you're a guest of Dave. They'll call me to the front and I'll walk you right on in." He pulls out a pen, writes something on a business card, and hands it to me.

All that's printed on it is the word "Bliss" on the front; his name's written there too, and there's an address on the back that he wrote down. The address is in a business area, so it's not his house. I have no idea what this is all about, so I stammer, "We'll see."

"Okay. All I ask is that you give it a chance. If you come by and don't want to stay, that'll be okay. But I think the adventurous side of you will like it. Bring your friend too. She might like it there."

"Thanks. Maybe I'll come by." There's something magnetic about this guy, something that makes me want to get to know him better. I start to think it might be time to leave, so I stand. He was right – the room *has* stopped moving. "I think I'd better get home before I'm tempted to get trashed again." I smile at him.

"It's been nice to meet you, Trish. I hope to see you again, maybe tomorrow night." He stands like a gentleman would. I have this overwhelming desire to hug him and, before the thought can go into and come back out of my brain, Dave says, "You're having a rough time. I'll give you a hug if you'd like." He opens his arms and for reasons I don't understand, I walk into his embrace. It feels comfortable and warm, not at all creepy. I really, really like this guy, and I make my mind up immediately. When he turns loose, I look up at him.

"It's been nice to meet you too, Dave. I'll see you tomorrow night." I turn and head home, Party Pooper in tow.

"What was that about?" Sheila quizzes me in the car.

"We've got somewhere to go tomorrow night," I tell her. Before I left the bar, I'd already made up my mind.

If there was adventure to be had there, I was going to plant myself right in the middle of it.

"I've got to work late."

"How late?" Sheila's backing out on me. I think she's scared.

"Until at least ten." She doesn't sound the least bit apologetic.

"Okay. Guess I'll go alone."

"No! That doesn't seem very smart, Trish. You don't know what you're walking into," she scolds into the phone.

"I'll be fine. It's in a business district in town. It'll be okay. But I wish you could go."

"Maybe another time. I'll talk to you tomorrow. I want to hear all about it." We hang up and I'm alone. The idea of going alone is kind of scary, but it's also kind of exciting too.

I'm in the bathroom, paying special attention to my makeup and hair, when I hear the front door open. It's got to be Ron.

Before I even make it into the room I yell out, "What the hell are you doing here?" It makes me furious to see him standing in the middle of the living room.

"I came by to pack up some more of my stuff. It's not like you're going anywhere." He finally takes a good look at me, and he looks surprised. "You're not, are you?"

"Actually, I am," I tell him and head back to the bathroom.

"And where are you going?" he asks. I want to tell him that it's none of his business, but that wouldn't be nearly as satisfying.

"Somewhere fun. To have an adventure." I'm trying not to grin too big.

"An adventure. I see. Well, you have fun with that." He doesn't sound convinced.

"I plan to. If you take anything that's not yours, so help me god, I'll chase you down and . . ."

"I won't. I just want this to be over, Trish. I've wasted too much time in this relationship."

Wow. I can't think of anything he could've said that would've hurt me more. I was wasted time. And he didn't waste mine? "Well, I'm done wasting my time on *you*. I'm going out and paint the town."

"Good luck. You wouldn't know fun if it bit you in the ass," he laughs.

Oh yeah? I'll show him. As least I hope I do.

I use my navigation system to find the address. When I get there, it's a nondescript building between two other buildings in a downtown block. There's a public parking garage across the street, so I park there and walk across.

There's no signage on the building until I walk up to the door. There's a small brass placard that says "BLISS." Nothing else. And it's only about a foot wide, so you have to be right in front of the door to see it. I stand there for a few seconds, then push on the door.

I step into something that looks strangely like a doctor's waiting room – fluorescent lighting, wood and vinyl chairs, and an office with a window. There's a guy sitting in the office and he looks like no physician's receptionist I've ever seen. He's got so much ink on him that he looks like a road map of Dallas, no kidding. He gives me a warm smile that looks kind of out of place on his face and says, "Hi! Can I help you?"

"Uh, yeah." I stumble over my own tongue and pull out the card. "Dave gave me this last night. He asked me to come by."

"Cleaning crew? Bartender?"

I'm confused. "Neither. Just a guest, I suppose."

"Oh! I'm sorry! I thought maybe you were here for a job or something." Sounds like just another club. "Let me call Dave up here." I walk around and look at the waiting room while he makes the call. It's all pretty plain. There are Ladies' Home Journal magazines in the magazine racks. That seems unusual at a club. The door to the back pops open and I hear Dave's voice.

"Trish! I'm so glad you came! Wow, you look nice!" That's the first compliment a man's paid me in, hell, I don't know how long.

"Thanks! You look pretty fine yourself!" I grin back, and then I'm kind of embarrassed. He picks up on it and hugs me again, and just like before, I feel at home in his arms.

"Come on in. And don't let the looks of the place fool you. It's as benign as you want it to be. I found you some stuff to wear. We have a locker room. Let me show you around." He opens the door and motions for me to go through.

The little hallway is kind of dark, but then it opens into a larger room.

And I wish the floor could open up and swallow me.

There are bare-breasted women everywhere, and a lot of them are wearing leather or rubber below their waists. Most of the guys are bare-chested, and they've all got on some kind of leather too. Some of the women are barefoot, but some wear boots or stilettos. There are tattoos everywhere in here, and piercings, and jewelry, and makeup. Some of the women are wearing elaborate, close-fitting necklaces, and I wonder about those, especially when I see that most have tiny padlocks on the backs of them. That's strange. I've forgotten that I'm moving until I bump into Dave as he stops at a doorway. "Locker room. Here." He hands me a brown paper bag. "Just choose an empty locker to stow your stuff. If you need help, just ask any lady in there. They'll be glad to help you. See you when you come out!" He pats my shoulder and walks away, so I go into the locker room, sit down on a bench, and start pulling out the things he's brought for me.

They're all brand-new. There's a lace tee. There's also an honest-to-god, lace-up corset; I assume that's to wear over the tee. The corset looks very expensive, with jewels and nail heads and embroidery, and it's beautiful. Skin-tight leggings are next, and they don't look like they'll fit, but they're stretchy, so I won't know for sure until I try them on. In the bottom of the bag is a pair of five-inch stilettos, Mary Jane-style with a platform, and they're sort of cute.

And did I mention it's all black? Everything's black.

I look around for a dressing room, but the only thing I see are a few showers. I wonder what I'm supposed to do when a woman who looks to be in her thirties wanders into the locker room.

"Wow! Nice fetwear! Where'd you get that corset?" She takes it from the bench and scrutinizes it. "This is amazing."

"Um, Dave," I start. "Do you know Dave?"

"Everybody does! Dave got this stuff for you? You're one lucky woman! He's got excellent taste, if you know what I mean!" I have no idea what she means. "Need some help with that?"

"Yeah, I will, but I can't find a dressing room." I motion around the room.

She gives me a funny look. "Why do you need one? I mean, rip it all off, girlfriend!" With that, she reaches down, grabs the hem of her tee shirt, and pulls it up and off. She's wearing absolutely nothing under it, and her breasts are only slightly droopy, with big nipples sporting gold rings. She proceeds to pull off everything, then reaches into a locker and starts getting dressed. When she's done, she's wearing a red leather thong, red leather garter belt, red stockings, and red stiletto-heeled boots, but she's wearing nothing on the top.

"Come on, let's get you dressed," she tells me. My pants come down and I pull the leggings on. She nods. "Looking good. Better put the shoes on. You may not be able to bend over once you get the corset on." There's considerable doubt in my mind that I can walk in the things, but I put them on anyway. She points to my boobs, so I pull my tee up and off. "Get that bra off," she barks, and I unhook it and take it down. I feel very self-conscious standing there, naked from the waist up, but she looks at me and says, "Nice tits! Here, put the lace tee on." I pull it on over my bare breasts and she holds up the corset. "Let's get this on you and I'll tie the laces." Corset in hand, she wraps it around me, zips the side, then grabs the laces and pulls it tight – too tight. I can barely breathe. "I know what you're going to say, but you'll get used to it. It makes your waist look smaller and makes you look very sexy."

When it's tied, she takes me to a mirror in the shower area. "Look! You look fabulous!" I see her pointing in the mirror and I take a look.

I barely recognize myself. I look, well . . .

Sexy. And adventurous.

She looks in the bag Dave handed me and says, "Yep, I thought you'd forgotten something." In the bottom in a small box are earrings and two bracelets, all of very delicate silver. They're all filigree and very large, and I'm touched at the trouble Dave went to for me.

When I've got the jewelry on, the woman says, "Oh, by the way, I'm Delilah. I'm a regular here. Are you a member?"

I shake my head. "I'm Trish and no, I just met Dave last night and he invited me to come."

"He's a wonderful person." She gets a serious look on her face, kind of like the one Dave wore the night before. "Have you ever been to a fetclub?"

"A what?"

"Um-hum. That answers my question. Look, if you have any questions about anything that's going on, just ask someone. They don't mind explaining. But don't interrupt them when they're doing a scene, okay? That's just poor form. A Dom needs to concentrate on his sub when they're scening."

"I have no idea what you just said," I tell her with a shrug.

"That's okay. You'll figure it out pretty quick. And remember: At Bliss, you don't have to do anything you don't want to. Safe, sane, and consensual, always. Ready?" She holds out her arm to me like she's going to escort me.

"I guess so. I have no idea what I'm supposed to be ready for." There's more going on here than I know or understand, and I'm terrified, but I'm also excited. And that's when, as I take her arm, she says the magic words.

"Well then, come on out and start the adventure."

There are strange sounds coming from the big room as we walk out into the hallway and head back into the light. When my eyes adjust to the lighting, I'm speechless.

There are three alcoves. In the farthest one, a woman is kneeling on some kind of bench, her forearms and wrists bound down with straps and her ass in the air, the bench turned so that her side is to the audience. And she's completely naked. A man stands to one side of her, facing the crowd, and he has what looks like some kind of whip in his hand. As I watch, he begins to lash her backside and she cries out, but she also has a peaceful look on her face.

In another small alcove, a woman is bound to a big cross-like apparatus, face out toward the crowd. There's a clamp on each of her nipples, and it looks excruciating. A chain runs from clamp to clamp, and a third chain hangs from the center of that one and runs down her stomach. It goes all the way down to her . . . oh, god, there's a clamp there too. How can she stand that? As she's standing there, the man with her is getting out something that looks like a microphone. But he hits a switch on it and it hums to life. It's a giant vibrator, and he presses it right into her slit. She shrieks and pants and, within a couple of minutes, she's having an orgasm, right there in front of everybody.

There's another alcove, a bigger one, and I can't see what's going on in there because of all the people crowded around. Whatever it is must be popular. When we walk up, one of the men says, "Oh, excuse me, subs. Hey, gentlemen, subs coming through." The crowd parts with his words, and Delilah and I walk right up to the front. That's when I stifle a gasp.

There's a woman, naked, on her back, strapped to a table. Arms, legs, everything, tied down, and there's a split in the table so that her legs are apart, leaving room between them to just walk up. There's red wax all over her, her breasts, chest, ribs, arms, legs, belly, privates, everywhere, obviously dripped on her while it was hot. Some kind of cords are tied around her nipples, their ends crossed across her body and tied to a d-ring on either side of the table so that there's a constant tension on them. And the pain from the cords is probably intensified with any movement. Which there is. There can't help but be movement.

Because the man in the alcove is fucking her. Right there. Right in front of everybody. His cock is unusually large and hard, and he's really giving it to her. I'm shocked, but no one around me seems to be the least bit fazed by it. Then I realize something kind of scary.

Deep down, while I stand there watching, I acknowledge to myself with great shame that I'm wishing I were her.

"Any questions?" Dave has poured me a cosmo and I'm sitting at the bar with him. He's not the bartender. He's something else much more important because everyone seems to defer to him in everything.

"Yeah. Do you own this place?" I have a lot of questions I'd like to ask, but I'm a little too embarrassed to ask them.

He laughs. "God, no! I'm just a very active member." After another swallow of the bourbon he's drinking, he says, "Very active. Leadership."

"Oh. I thought maybe you . . ." And I'm too embarrassed to finish.

"What? Try out all of the subs? I wish!" he chuckles. "Nah. I have a couple I play with on a regular basis, but that's about it." I'm trying to figure out what a sub is and what they call play. "So you watched the scenes. Any questions about any of that?"

It's hard to look at him. "Well, I guess I, what I don't understand is, I mean . . ." I stammer.

"Look, Trish, I know that was probably pretty shocking to you. But we're all very open about our sex lives around here, and we're not shy about our sexuality. There's no shame here. Look around. Most of these people have bodies that are far from perfect." That was true; I'd noticed a few of them and thought to myself that I'd *never* take my clothes off in public if I looked like that. But they seem completely comfortable. I have to admire that.

"So what's the purpose of all this? Why can't they just do this at home?"

"First, the equipment is too expensive and takes up too much room." That makes sense. "Second, some people actually like to be viewed when they're doing this. They enjoy it and find it arousing." I can't even imagine that. "And third, not everyone has someone at home to play with." Ah. Playing equals sex.

"But the people who were doing the scenes, they're married, right?"

"Gosh no!" He laughs outright at that question. "The guy with the flogger? He and that sub play together all the time, but they're not attached, just negotiate as they go along. The couple fucking in the big alcove," he says, not even flinching at the word, "are in a committed D/s relationship." I have no idea what that means. "But the woman with the clamps? This is the first time she's been here."

I gasp. "She's never done this before?"

He shakes his head. "No, no, no, that's not what I mean. She's in the lifestyle. She's a member of another club in another city, but she's in town on business and had some needs. She came here looking for a service Dom to, well, service her. And Master Justin stepped up to the plate. That may or may not include sex; doesn't always."

"So she just came in here and asked someone to do that?"

"Yes. They negotiated what they'd be doing before they started. If I'm not mistaken, they're in a private room right now." He smiles and takes another sip of bourbon.

"You mean they're back there . . ."

"Fucking? Yeah. I certainly hope so, because we don't have enough private rooms to go around, and I'd hate to think there are other people who'd like to be back there fucking and those two are in there playing gin rummy or something," he chuckles. "Want another drink?"

"No, but I need one." My face is burning in embarrassment, and Dave gets the bartender to hand me another glass full of fortitude.

He looks at me for a minute, then says, "I want to ask you something. And I want you to be honest with me."

"Okay. I'll try." I take another big swig of my drink. I'm afraid I'm going to need more.

"I have to believe that there was at least a moment while you were watching those scenes in which you wished you were the sub in the scene. Am I right?" Those big blue eyes bore right into me. In my humiliation, it feels like he's looking right through my skin and into my insides, and I shiver. "Well?"

I'm sure my face is purple, and I feel sweat beads pop up on my upper lip. But I nod. "Yes. At least once." My eyes can't meet his.

I feel something on my chin and the next thing I know, Dave pulls my face up and looks me right in the eyes. My stomach drops. "Trish, don't be ashamed. Your feelings are completely normal – for you. If you have those needs, this is the place to have them met. There's nothing wrong with you and nothing wrong with this. Just feel the feelings and let them lead you to what you need. And I'll be here to help you in your adventure."

My mind snaps and I blurt out, "So if you don't own this place, exactly what *is* your role here?"

Dave laughs and turns loose of my chin. "Little sub, I'm the dungeon master."

The rest of the evening passes quickly, primarily because I'm in a state of shock. I see things I didn't think I'd ever see, including a gorgeous guy licking the boots of one of the homeliest women I've ever seen while calling her his "supreme mistress." That's an eye-opener. And I notice something else very strange – well, strange to me anyway.

"Dave?"

"Yeah, little one?"

"There are lots of guys around here without women. Some of them keep looking at me, but none of them are coming over to talk to me. Are they gay?" I'm used to being hit on at bars, but I'm not extremely attractive, and these guys are. We're talking really, *really* hot.

"Nope. They're not gay. Well, a couple of them may be bi." He stops for a second and my eyebrows shoot up. "But that's not it. You're new. They're watching. They don't want to offend you by being too forward. I'm sure the oldest ones in the bunch have figured out that you're not in the lifestyle, and they don't want you to feel uncomfortable. They're not staring, are they?"

"Nope. They're just sneaking glances." It's kind of funny.

"That's what I thought. Plus you're not collared." Ah. Those funny necklaces with the padlocks. "They're afraid you're in here looking for a Dom, and most of them just want to play, not collar a sub." I assume that collaring is some kind of relationship. That makes sense to me.

I decide to throw some furtive glances their way. One of the guys is tall and blond, Viking-like in his coloring and build. There are a couple of guys with medium-brown hair and nice tans, but they look like hard workers, not beach bums spending their days lying out in the sun for the hell of it. Maybe construction workers. Or cowboys. Just nice guys. And there's another guy.

He didn't stand out at first. When he glances my way, I look away. There's something about his eyes, like they want to devour me. He's good-looking enough, wavy chestnut brown hair and a nice build, not heavy or stocky, just muscular, probably barely over six feet tall. I'll be fifty next year; he looks to be maybe forty? But there's something about his face, his eyes actually, that just draws me in. I turn to Dave.

"Hey, who's the guy over there alone? The one with the eyes."

Dave looks at me like I'm nuts, then glances over my shoulder. "Oh, that's Master Clint. He's had a rough couple of years. I'm trying to get him to look for a sub to collar, but he's resistant. Has his hands full."

"Full of what?" Now I'm curious.

"You'd have to ask him," Dave tells me, and I swear I see the corners of his mouth turn up just the tiniest bit. I feel like he's just issued me a challenge and I'm trying to decide if I accept. "Think you'll come back?" he asks, interrupting my reverie.

"I'd like to. Can I?"

"Sure! I'll work out something with the membership fee. And I'll volunteer to be your trainer if you want." He's not smiling, just looking at me like he's waiting for me to decide.

Then it hits me. "Does that mean we'll be having sex at some point?"

"I don't know any other way to train a sub so, yes, I'm sure we will."

There's a second or two when I think I'm going to say no and then, to my surprise, I say, "Yeah. Sure. You can be my trainer." *Where the hell did that come from?*, my vacationing brain screams. "What exactly does it mean to train me?"

"There's really no training per se. It's just a process of helping you understand the lifestyle before you come out here and start to get requests to scene, get some idea of what a Dom would expect from you both submissively and sexually, and to help you decide if you'd like to be collared at some point. Still interested?"

"Absolutely." I can't believe I'm saying this. But I was looking for adventure, right? I'm pretty sure I've found it.

"Okay. I'll work up some kind of schedule for training and give it to you to look over. It'll probably take me a few days. In the meantime, get yourself tested and bring in the results." At first I think he means for drugs, and then I realize what he's talking about.

"I haven't been with anyone except my husb . . . ex in upwards of thirty years."

"Yeah, but do you know where *he's* been that entire time?" I see his point, and I shake my head. "So get tested just to be on the safe side. Then we can proceed. Until then, if sex comes up in your training, we've got plenty of condoms around here. Shouldn't be a problem." He says it so matter-of-factly that you'd think he fucks some new sub trainee every day.

Well, maybe he does. "Have very many subs you're training?"

Dave laughs. He really looks sexy when he does that. "Nope, little one. I haven't trained a sub in eight years. And I'm not sure I want to train you, but I am sure of one thing: I don't want you getting hurt or scared. As long as I'm training you, I know you're safe. So I'm willing to do it. Plus," he says and winks, "you look like a good fuck."

Have to admit, no one's ever said *that* to me before, and I kind of like it.

Chapter 2

After I get home, I lie in bed, staring at the ceiling and trying to digest everything I saw and heard. I also can't get Master Clint's face out of my mind. There's something about those eyes, the intensity of his gaze and the sadness there, that I can't shake. I'm wondering if I'll ever meet him.

The next day, Sheila tries every ploy she can think of to get me to tell her where I went and what I did. I won't. I think she's mad. Too bad. She could've come along too, but she backed out – work, my ass.

So I start doing some thinking, and I work through lunch so I can take off an hour early. When I leave the office, I go straight to the place named on the front of the bag that Dave had handed me. And I'm not disappointed when I get there.

All they have is – what do they call it? fetwear? – and it's almost overwhelming. There's a young girl with pink, spikey hair working, hanging up things that I can't bring myself to call clothes. I guess she sees me looking around and she comes up to me quietly, so quietly that when she speaks, I jump about a foot. "Can I help . . . oh, gee, I didn't mean to scare you! Can I help you find something?"

What should I say to her?, I wonder. She doesn't know me, so I decide to just jump right in. "Yeah, um, I'm joining a fetish club and I'm going to be going through sub training. And I'm not," I look at her and smile, "your age. So what would you suggest for someone like me?"

"Honey, if you're joining a fetclub, it doesn't matter how old you are. Nobody in the club scene cares about age. So tell me, what's the fetish? Is this a foot club? A tit club? An ass club? A BDSM club?"

"BDSM?"

"Yeah. Bondage-discipline-sadism-masochism-dominance-submission-slave-master." She says it so easily that I'm pretty sure that's what she's up to in her free time.

"That's it." I make a mental note to look it up on the Internet and learn that term. If I'm going to do it, I should be fluent in it. "So I need to know what to wear, and I need to buy some things. I don't want to wear the same thing every time I go."

"Some people do. Fetwear is kind of expensive, so some people *have* to wear the same thing every time. One outfit will set you back a couple hundred dollars." I think she sees the look of horror on my face because she's quick to add, "But I think I can help you with some mix-and-match stuff that will work out nicely and be a little cheaper."

We start to go through the racks. I find a black and red leather corset that I like a lot. She finds a black lace tank and a black, ruffled, short skirt to go with it. I have the leggings Dave gave me and that corset, plus the black lace tee. She finds me a pair of boots that I really like, mid-calf with buckles up the sides and four-inch heels. I pick through a rack and find a dark purple leather bra with an attached, sheer flounce that reaches down past my waist. That's really, really cute. She comes up with some leather shorts, and then I find purple shoes. Bingo. She rings it all up and it's two hundred and forty-some-odd dollars, but I think that's a steal. I put it all on Ron's credit card. He doesn't know it, but he's going to pay for it.

On my way out, I notice some jewelry. It's beautiful. I mean, I know the stones aren't real, and it's just cheap metal, but it's nice for the club scene. She's showing me some pretty pieces that will work with what I've bought when I move down a case and see something that takes my breath away.

The case is full of collars. Some of them are plain wide leather, and some are chain. There are a couple of thin silver ones, a few thin leather, and there's one or two made of brass. But right in the middle of the group is a piece that makes my heart almost stop.

It's gold, gleaming gold, and about an inch wide. It has a row of stones along the top and bottom of the band, but right in the center, it has a cluster of stones that form a heart, and the heart is also filled in with stones. It's gorgeous. It even has a stone-encrusted gold padlock, and the keys for it have a heart-shaped cutout for the key ring to run through. She sees me staring at it and takes it out of the case.

"It's beautiful, isn't it?" she sighs, and I can tell she's wishing she had someone to give it to her.

"They're not real, are they?"

"They absolutely are." She turns the price tag over and I start to laugh.

"Might as well put that back. It won't be on my neck anytime soon."

"Yeah, but put it on and see how it looks! I haven't had the balls to." She pulls a mirror on a stand over to me, then takes the collar out of the case and hands it to me.

I'm afraid of bending it out of shape, but it's hinged. It's much lighter-weight than it looks. I put it on, push it together in the back, and lean over to the mirror.

I went the extra mile with my hair and makeup this morning because I wanted to look good this evening. When I look in the mirror, I can't believe my eyes. I look . . .

Beautiful?

I look like a princess. It's amazing. My eyes start to tear, and the girl says, "Oh my god, you look stunning in that! You're kind of glowing!" I can't help it; I start to cry outright. Would any man ever see what I just saw in that mirror? Or will they just see a middle-aged woman who's boring, and tedious, and uninteresting?

I take the collar off, thank her, and hurry out of the store. I'm going home, and I'll get ready and go to the club. Maybe one of the guys there will ask me to play.

"Well, don't you look lovely?" Dave says in greeting when I get to the club. "Looks like you went shopping!"

"Yeah! Like it?" I twirl for him in the cute little skirt and the purple bra-thing. The purple shoes look nice with it.

"Yeah, just one problem." He takes me by the elbow and leads me back to the locker room area, then points through the doorway. "Underwear."

"I put on my best ones . . ."

"Not allowed. Take them off. Then come back out to the bar. I'll be waiting." He turns and walks away without another word.

I drag myself into the locker room and pull off my panties. Trying to figure out what to do with them, I stuff them in my purse and my purse in a locker, and use the combination lock I brought with me to secure it all. When I go back out to the bar, I feel like everyone in the place can tell I don't have on any underwear. Then I realize that the other women most likely aren't wearing any either. At the bar, Dave doesn't say anything. He just motions for me to turn around backward. Once my back is to him, he reaches down and pulls up my skirt, right there at the bar. Before I can protest, he drops it and says, "Better. Now, we need to sit down and go over this training schedule."

His hand grabs mine and he leads me over to a leather sofa. Instead of sitting, I just stand there, not sure what to do but pretty sure nobody wants my bare ass sitting on the sofa. Quick as a wink, he says, "Sorry!" and reaches over to a table next to the sofa. There's a stack of towels there, and he drapes one onto the sofa, then motions for me to sit. Problem solved. Apparently that's pretty common around here too.

"You need to know that there's really no such thing as 'training' a sub. Each Dom has his own likes and expectations, so they pretty much do their own training once you've got a contract. This is just a manner of introducing you to the lifestyle and letting you become accustomed to the most common things a Dom will expect. That way you can kind of determine if this is really something you want. So here's what I came up with."

We look over the schedule. Apparently under his tutelage I'm expected to learn to give oral sex, get oral sex, comply with various types of bondage and discipline, use sensory perception while blindfolded, follow orders, and have anal sex. I will be undergoing orgasm denial, orgasm torture, and various types of deprivation. I have no idea what that means, but I'm sure I'll find out. While we work together, I'm to call him "Sir," and when we're scening together, I'm to call him "Master;" that's easy enough. We will use every piece of equipment in the house, and he'll also be using all kinds of toys on me. That should be interesting. Mattel and Fisher-Price come to mind, but I'm pretty sure they don't make these kinds of toys.

"So at which of these times will we be having sex?" I ask. I want to be prepared.

"For any of these training sessions, if you have a clitoral orgasm, you'll *want* to have sex. Otherwise, it's at my discretion."

"I'm trusting you to be discreet. Sir." Dave smiles, and I feel better about the whole thing.

"And I'll be training your body to come on command."

"I'll already be there," I say, confused.

"No, come." Then it sinks in and I know what he means.

"On command?" That sounds impossible.

"Yes. You'll hear my voice and you'll immediately get aroused and wet. And when I tell you to, you'll come, have an orgasm. It'll take a while, but you'll get there. Then the trick will be to transfer that ability to a Dom when you take one."

"You mean when he takes me, right?"

"Different clubs and Doms do it different ways. Some have the sub offer the collar. We typically have the Dom offer it. There will be a ceremony, and the sub stands and is offered for collaring. If a Dom thinks he can be the one she needs, he'll come forward and offer to collar her. She can choose to accept or decline. If she accepts, he'll offer her his collar. Usually, if the sub thinks he can be the Dom she needs, she'll accept it." Dave smiles. I have to wonder if he ever had a long-term sub.

"But doesn't love have anything to do with it?" It seems to me that it should.

"It doesn't have to, little one. But it's wonderful when it does."

Then I think of something else. "Why were you in that bar? I mean, you have a nice one here? Why were you there the other night?"

He gives me a little grin. "I have no idea. I was just walking by on my way from the bank and I thought it looked like an interesting little place. Turned out to be very interesting!"

I stop for a second and look into his face. "Dave, why are you doing this? Why would you waste all this time on me?"

He smiles and puts a hand on my cheek. "Any time I spend with you won't be wasted. When I saw you at the bar, I knew you were a born submissive, could just tell. You aren't boring – you were just waiting for someone to take the reins and challenge you. You're a diamond in the rough when it comes to your skills. But I don't think it'll take much to turn you into a sub any Dom would be proud to collar." When a tear forms in my eye, he says, "I don't think you have any idea how special you are."

He's right. I sure don't. And I think *he's* crazy for thinking that, but I like to hear him say it anyway.

I see the chestnut-haired Dom standing across the room by the bar when I come out of the private room where Dave and I had been meeting. Before I left, Dave told me to lie down on the bed and spread my legs so he could have a look at me. I felt like I was in the gynecologist's office. He opened my folds with his fingers, gave my clit a few strokes, then pumped a finger into me a couple of times. He brushed his hands along my skin, pulled down the straps of my bra, then the cups, and toyed with my nipples for a minute. It was turning me on and I was almost hoping he'd offer to have sex with me, but he didn't. Instead, he said, "You look great. I'll enjoy working with you," then helped me up off the bed and slapped me on the ass as I walked out the door. "Tomorrow night. Don't be late." I nodded, then came out here. And that's when I saw him.

I head straight to the bar, not to him. Well, actually, I *am* heading straight to him, but that's not something he has to know. I order my customary cosmo and turn like I'm looking around. Our eyes meet and he almost smiles, then turns those dark eyes away.

The cosmo is delivered. Drink in hand, I walk down the bar toward him. When I'm at the stool next to his, I say, "Excuse me, is this seat taken?"

He turns like I've shot him and blurts out, "No, it's not." And as quickly as the words come out, he spins and walks away.

I stand there, wondering if my breath is horrible or something. But before I have a chance to do or say anything, a body moves up next to me and sits down.

It's the Viking.

"Hello there." He holds out his right hand. "My name is Steffen. And you're . . ."

"Patricia. Trish." I take his hand and shake it. Instead of turning it loose, he takes his other hand and puts it on top of mine.

"It's a pleasure. I've haven't seen you in here. New?"

"Yes. Completely. Untrained." At that word, I see his eyes light up and his smile deepen.

"Untrained! Well, well, well. Looking for someone to train you?"

"She's got someone, Steffen," I hear Dave's voice say.

"I didn't realize she was taken," Steffen says quickly.

"She's not. If you want to play with her, know that I'll be asking what you did and how you did it. I don't want her hurt or scared in any way, understand?" My chest feels warm when I realize that an older, experienced Dom wants to protect me.

"I would never do that. Only what she's comfortable with." Steffen turns from Dave back to me. "Would you like to play?"

Dave told me about negotiating. "Depends on what that entails." I'm starting to feel a little frisky.

"How about I just concentrate on doing something that would please you but would be a little challenging for you? How does that sound?" I like his smile. It's just warm enough with an edge of danger, and I find it thrilling.

"That sounds pretty good." I throw a glance at Dave to see what his reaction is, and he smiles and nods. This Steffen guy must be okay.

"We'll take the alcove on the right. It's not in use." He tries to lead me to it, but I sit back on my heels.

"In front of everybody?" There's panic blooming in my stomach.

"Yes. In front of everybody." He stops and looks into my face. "One of the most important things the Dom tries to propagate in his sub is trust. Do you trust me? Have I done anything that would make you distrust me?"

There's no retort for that. "No, I don't guess you have."

"Then trust me to make this a positive experience?"

I nod. "Okay. I'll try." My voice is shaky, but I'm feeling resolved and I want to do a good job as a first-time sub. When we're out of earshot of Dave, I lean up to Steffen and whisper, "Can I ask you something?"

"Of course. Anything. If it's too personal, I'll tell you." He's getting ready to perform some kind of sexual act on me in front of a group of people and there's something too personal for him to share with me?

"No. Nothing like that. It's just . . . what does 'sub' mean?"

I'm pretty sure he'll laugh at me, but that's not what he does. He pulls me to a sofa instead, spreads out another towel, and pats it with his hand for me to sit. "I'm a Dom – a Dominant. That's the character trait with which I most identify. It's in my nature to be dominating, but with that comes the responsibility to care for my sub in a way that will allow her, or him, to love and trust me, to look to me to have his or her needs met." I nod.

"I call you a submissive. There's something in your nature that responds to a strong, capable Dominant. You know that for your sexual fulfillment to be complete, you need to submit to someone who can and will fulfill your every sexual fantasy. You will trust that person to take care of you while still pushing your boundaries safely so that you achieve levels of sexual satisfaction that you couldn't in regular vanilla sex." I'd heard about that vanilla thing – I read the trilogy. "Does that all make sense?"

I nod again. "Thanks. That seemed to be the simplest thing in the world for everyone else, but I just didn't understand."

"Sometimes we overlook the obvious while moving toward the complex. Simple things matter too. They're the building blocks of trust and submission."

This guy is smart. And damn sexy. I decide that whatever he wants to do in that alcove, I'm going to trust him.

Steffen leads me back up to the stage area in the alcove and says simply, "Sub, present yourself to your master." I have no idea what that means. I walk toward him and he sweetly says, "Kneel." When I get to my knees, he says, "Arch your back so your breasts push forward." When I do, he says, "A little more." I try again. "Much better. Now, turn your hands palms up and rest the backs of your hands on your thighs." That was easy, and I hear him say, "Beautiful. Now, bow your head, but don't let the arch in your back fade." I try to do what he's said. "Arch your back a little more. A little more. There! That's beautiful. Good job." I feel sort of like a dog, except there's no treat. I'm hoping I'll get that in a few minutes. He gives me a moment or two to settle into the pose. While I'm doing so, he says, "Holding the pose like that will help your muscles build memory for it. It's uncomfortable for you now, but as you practice it, it will become more comfortable until you enjoy sitting in this manner." Then he adds, "And it's important that you begin to learn to not look a Dom in the eye unless asked to. When trusting a Dom to care for you, you should reciprocate with respect."

I cast my eyes downward and answer with a simple, "Yes, Master." He says nothing, so I assume he's pleased.

After what seems like an eternity, he says, "Rise. Gracefully." I try and I think I do a pretty good job. "Work on that, but it was good for a first time. Give me your hand." Careful not to look into his face, I hold my right hand out and he takes it in his left, then leads me to a piece of equipment.

He turns to me with his back to the crowd and very quietly says, "Lie down with your torso along the beam, a breast on either side. Put your hands down by the front legs of the horse. I'll position your legs." I lie down on the horse just like he said and, to my horror, both of my breasts pop out of my bra-thing. I wait for the laughter; it doesn't come. That breast thing must happen pretty often around here. When I put my hands down, he secures them to the front legs of the horse with cuffs that are already in place. This is starting to make me nervous. I feel him take hold of each of my ankles and fasten them in place on the platforms to either side of the horse. I'm bound to the horse and helpless. And, oddly, it feels, well . . . it's very arousing. He turns the horse so my ass is away from the crowd, and I remember that I don't have on any underwear. I have to be sure to thank him and Dave for that.

He walks to the front, squats down, and fondles both of my nipples. I feel the heat rising in my cheeks but, to my surprise, it's pooling between my legs as well. My nipples are getting harder and harder to the point that they're aching. I know everyone is watching and, as though he can hear my thoughts, Steffen whispers to me, "Don't worry about anyone but me. As long as you're pleasing me, I'll please you."

"Yes, Master," I think to say.

"Very good, pretty thing." He stands and moves behind me and addresses the audience. "Tonight we'll do a little orgasm denial. This can be useful in discipline. There's nothing more frustrating to a sub than to be brought to the edge, only to be left hanging without satisfaction. I'll stroke her clit and watch for the signs." Signs? I'm not sure what he's talking about.

His fingers graze my slit, and then he parts my lips with two fingers and finds my bud. It's aching. "Your tiny little dick is hard as a rock, pretty one," he murmurs to me and begins to stroke rhythmically. Suddenly, I realize that I've forgotten about all of the people watching, I've forgotten to be embarrassed, and I've forgotten to be worried about what he thinks about my naked backside. All I'm thinking about is the next second and how good it'll feel as compared to this one. I feel the tension building in my belly, feel my hips start to rock, and I start to moan. I'm right at the edge, and I start to tell him that I'm going to come when . . .

He stops.

I wail. When I do, he slaps my bare ass. "None of that. Be a good girl, not a brat. Take it like a good sub." I'm shaking with need, and I can't do anything about it. If I could get my hands free, I'd stroke myself, but I can't.

He starts again. This time, I'm more sensitive and it doesn't take as long. His fingers are talented, and a sweat breaks out on my brow. My stomach muscles are starting to clench, and I feel the muscles in my pussy clenching too. The orgasm is right on me, about to overtake me.

And he stops again.

This time I manage to stifle my groan, but my hips are still churning and I feel like I'm on fire. "Much better, pretty one. Once more." He slaps my ass again, then takes his hand and slaps my entire pussy. The blood rushes to the impact points, and I can almost feel myself swelling.

His finger moves to my most sensitive area again and starts to methodically stroke, this time around and around the glans of my clit. I'm almost screaming, but I'm quiet. It's a struggle, though. The circling is driving me mad, and my hips are bucking. I can see my breasts hanging down either side of the horse and bouncing as I writhe, and my nipples are so swollen that they look like flames might shoot out of them. Everything in my lower body is going into spasms, and I need relief. I'm getting closer, closer, so close, and I tense my legs, waiting for it to hit.

Of course, he stops.

That's it for me. I start to cry. I'm not sobbing out loud, but the tears are rolling down my face. They're hot and fast, and I don't know how much more of this I can take. He can see my shoulders shaking with sobs, I'm sure. He puts his hand on my lower back and I hear him whisper, "Pretty one, I'm very impressed. You're doing very, very well. We're almost there."

His hand moves back down my slit and, this time, I'm determined to hang in there. His finger finds its mark and he starts again, slowly, around my clit. My teeth find my lower lip and I bite it in an attempt to stay quiet. He's working my nub and my abdominal muscles are cramped and tight, my pussy in spasms, and my arms and legs rigid in their shackles. I feel faint and lightheaded, and I don't know what's going to happen. Working its way around, over and over, his finger doesn't just hit the magic spot, it's abrading it, torturing it, asking it to give in. Spots are beginning to form in the backs of my eyes, and I'm panting over my bitten lip. I'm not sure what's going to happen, but I'm going all in. Just as I feel the climax working its way through me, I feel Steffen's other hand rest gently on my ass cheek, almost like a caress, and he says the magic words.

"Pretty one, let go and come for me." He gives my clit an extra little flick, and everything inside me explodes. I know I'm shrieking, but I can't control it, and he keeps going until I'm straining against my restraints and jerking. Then he stops.

Before I can stop my tears, he's at my head, squatting in front of me. "Look at me, pretty one," he says, and I look up. He smiles into my face, leans down, and kisses me. I kiss him back, a hungry kiss, because now I know what Dave was trying to tell me: I want to be fucked. Right now. I need it.

Steffen has my restraints loose in just a few seconds, and he picks me up. That's a good thing, because I really don't think I could walk at this minute. Quick as a wink, I find myself in a big bed in a dimly-lit room, candles burning and soft music playing. There's a hand on my cheek and a sweet male voice says, "That was so good, pretty one. You did very well. I want to satisfy you. Would you like for your master to fuck you?"

There's no way for me to stop myself. "Yes, please! Please get inside me!"

"Use the words, sub. What do you want?"

I've never said anything like that out loud, and I don't know if I can, but I'm not going to get what I want if I don't try. "Please, oh please, screw . . ." He pinches my ass. "Oh god!" I pant. "Oh, please, I need you to . . . please . . . please fuck me! I need you to fuck me!" I can't believe those words are coming out of my mouth, and I can't believe I haven't said them before. They're so freeing, to ask for what I want and know that I'm going to get it.

"That's 'Master.' Call me Master, pretty one."

"Yes, please, Master! I need to be fucked, Master. Please?"

"Let's get you up where you'll really enjoy it." He manipulates my body like I'm a poseable doll, and in a few seconds I'm on my elbows and knees, ass in the air. "Arch your back to give me better access to your pussy, pretty one." I do as I'm told. "Perfect. I'll fuck you now. Please let me know if I'm satisfying you."

Juices are already dripping out of my cunt and running down my leg, and all it takes is the tiniest push from him and he's in me, stroking me, the parts of me no one's ever stroked that way. I've never been fucked this way, never felt so thoroughly used and so thoroughly sated. I want more, more, more.

"What do you need, pretty one?" Steffen pants.

"More, please, Master! I need more! Please fuck me harder!" It's almost like I'm having an out-of-body experience because I can't believe I'm begging to be fucked by a guy I didn't know an hour before.

He picks up the pace and my mind is going somewhere it's never been. Everything goes white, and every muscle in my body responds as I scream out my orgasm. I've never had a vaginal orgasm like this, and it's stupendous. There's nothing else like it, and I ride it for all it's worth.

Next thing I know, I'm in strong arms, snuggled tight to a big, broad chest. There's a hand stroking my hair, and I've never felt so safe. The sensation is almost like floating. I hear a calm, warm, male voice say, "Come down, pretty one. It's over. No more flying," and he chuckles.

"Can I look up at you now? Please?" I ask. I don't want to be called a brat again.

"Please do." The face I look up into is smiling back at me. "How was that?"

"I don't know." He shoots me a puzzled look. "I'd have to get a thesaurus, because I'm pretty sure 'awesome' is overused and I don't know what else to call it." He chuckles again. "That was incredible," I manage, then finish with, "Master."

"You're a quick study," he murmurs, then surprises me by kissing me. I kiss him back and stroke his cheek, and he wraps his hand around the back of my neck and kisses my forehead. "I think Dave is really going to enjoy training you. I'd like to get another shot at it too. Whaddya think?"

"I think that's absolutely, positively doable!" My grin is bound to be goofy, but I don't care. It's genuine. I've never felt like this in my life. Do I want to do this again?

Oh hell yeah.

Chapter 3

That was Wednesday night. On Thursday night, Dave works with me all evening. Everything that I suspected about the man is true. He's even more gorgeous naked, is the sexiest thing I've ever seen, and is as trustworthy and honest as they come. But he's really, really mad when I come through the door.

There's no mistaking it. First thing, he grabs me by the arm and drags me to a private room. Once there, he asks me point-blank, "Did Steffen tell you about safewording?" The look I give him must've answered his question, because now he's livid. "I can't believe that. He knows you're a novice. What the hell was he thinking?"

"Hey, Dave, really, no harm, no foul. I don't know what . . ."

"Safewording. You choose a word. If you call that word, all play stops. I was watching you up there scening. I know you would've called a safeword if you'd known to."

I shake my head. "No, I wouldn't have. I was enjoying myself. Well, as much as someone can enjoy being tortured. But there's no doubt in my mind, if I had cried out and asked Steffen to stop, he would've."

He's still angry, but that seems to have calmed him a bit. "Steffen and I will have a talk."

"Okay. But know that I thought the whole thing was unbelievably great, and I'd do it again in a heartbeat." I smile at him, and finally he smiles back.

"You may have to eat your words," he grins.

"I'll eat whatever you give me and ask for more," I grin back. In a split second, he presses me to my knees, then unzips his leathers. I find myself face to face with what has to be the mightiest cock I've ever seen. I get out one word: "Whoaaaa."

"Glad to see you approve. You give head?" he asks.

"I have, but not well. And not on demand."

"Well, you will now. Suck me, sub. Watch those teeth. And I'll give you direction. I expect you to follow it."

"Yes, Master."

"Very good. Take me in your mouth."

Only about five strokes in, he tells me, "I'm going down your throat. You're going to choke. There's no way around it. But if you'll pretend you're yawning every time I press in, you'll eventually get it. Don't worry about drool, tears, or snot; it's part of the process. This will be the first thing we practice every time you're here until you get it down pat. Fellatio is one of the things a Dom desires the most from his sub. It's the ultimate act of submission, especially when the sub swallows, and it's the one gift a Dom can give his sub that no other Dom can, that particular taste and smell that's all his. Some Dom is going to enjoy it from you, and you'll enjoy giving him this gift back."

As he spoke, I'd started to stroke down on him, but when he stops talking, he takes my head with both hands and shoves it down onto his thick shaft. I feel like someone has put a foot on my neck, and I could swear I'm seeing stars. When he pulls me off, he says, "Take a deep breath and down again." He repeats the process. By this point, I'm pretty sure he's trying to kill me. He shoves me back down over his cock and I gag again. This time, when he lifts my head, I'm coughing almost uncontrollably. "Again, little one." Just before his cock head hits my throat, I remember to try to yawn. That's all it takes; it goes right past my soft palate and down my throat, and I want to cheer. Except I can't. Because I've got a giant cock down my throat.

"Good girl!" he praises, then starts thrusting into my throat. It's not so terrible now that I can let it go on down, and he's really getting into it. I do hate the saliva that's falling from my lips and the fact that my eyes and nose are running profusely, but I can't help that. There's a sense of accomplishment on my part that I can't describe. This man has taken his time to train me, and I'm giving him something that's making him feel really, really good.

After a good five minutes, he says, "Reach up and fondle my balls. Gently. Like you'd roll billiard balls in your hand." I've never heard it described that way, and I try it. He moans – loudly. I take that to mean I'm doing it right. In under two minutes, I hear him groan, "I'm going to come down your throat. Spitting is disrespectful. I expect you to swallow." I'd nod, but I can't. His balls are still in my hand, and I feel them draw up just before he explodes in my mouth. There's so much cum that I'm having trouble swallowing it, but I manage.

Before I can catch my breath, he takes me by the upper arms and pulls me up. "Sorry I look such a sight," I whine, looking around for something to wipe my mouth, eyes, and nose with.

He hands me a towel. "I'd be concerned if everything wasn't running. That would be very abnormal. And the saliva is important, very needed, so you need to work *toward* that, not avoid it. But overall that was very good, little one. You're a quick learner."

"That's what Master Steffen said."

"I see he also told you not to look your Dom in the eye."

"Yes, Master."

"Very good. I'll have to thank him for that. Now, go lie on the bed and open yourself to me. I'm going to return the favor."

I do as I'm told and in just a few minutes, I'm riding an orgasmic wave that takes me to another world. Steffen is good; Dave is an expert. He knows just how to speed up and slow down to make the most of his work, and his hands and tongue are nothing short of miraculous. I'm impressed – and thankful.

"Are you coming back tomorrow?" he asks as he holds me after my orgasm.

"I was planning to unless you don't want me to."

He smiles. "Now why would I want you to stay away?"

I have to ask. "Do all of you always hold the subs, you know, afterward?" I know what I'm hoping he'll say.

"Absolutely. I don't know a respectable Dom who doesn't." He must be able to see the disappointment on my face; I was hoping I was special, but apparently I'm not. "Hey, listen, we do it because we genuinely care about you and your feelings. We don't want to treat you like whores, because you're not. You're here, giving yourself to men who love and respect women. We want you to feel special, not used and thrown aside. Let me put it this way," he says, stroking one of my nipples. "If you ever scene with a Dom who doesn't hold and cuddle you afterward, don't ever scene with him again. He's just using you. And you don't deserve that. You deserve to feel special, precious, cared for. Because you're all of those things to all of us. There's not a man in this club who wouldn't jack somebody up for calling you a name or hurting you in any way."

A tear rolls down my cheek, and Dave wipes it off. "Thanks," I manage to stammer. "I needed to have someone say that to me."

"You're welcome. And it's true." He kisses my forehead.

"Hey, can I ask you something?"

"Sure, baby."

"Do you think I'm boring?"

Dave lets loose a belly laugh. "Honey, you're a lot of things, but boring isn't one of them. Tomorrow night, I fuck your ass. And I guarantee the last thing I'll think is that you're boring!"

He's going to fuck my ass. I'm scared to death. And very, very excited.

I get a big surprise the next night when I get there. Big surprise. Really huge. Something I never could've expected.

"I've got a little emergency. I've got to go pick up my daughter and take her to the hospital. Her husband was hurt in an accident about fifteen minutes ago," Dave tells me absent-mindedly, and he's scurrying around the private room where we meet. "So I asked someone else to work with you tonight. I hope you don't mind, sweetie."

I shake my head. "If you trust him enough to ask, then I trust your judgment enough to trust him."

He nods. "This guy is the most trustworthy person I've ever met. I'd trust him with my life – and yours. He'll be here in about ten minutes, and he knows he's supposed to work with you. Just go on out to the bar and he'll come and get you."

"Who is . . ." Before I can ask, he's out the door.

I straggle back out to the bar and ask for a cosmo. I'm sitting there, listening to the music, inspecting my nails, when I hear someone say, "Trish? Aren't you Trish?"

I turn and I can't believe my eyes.

It's Clint.

All I can manage to stammer is, "Uh, yeah, Trish, um, yeah. Uh . . ."

He sticks out his hand for me to shake. "I'm Clint. Dave asked me to work with you tonight."

"Um, sure." My face is reddening. As I shake his hand, I can feel my cheeks burning. And I must look like a complete imbecile.

"So if you want to finish your drink in the private room, we can get started." I'm more than a little off kilter. He's being very professional about the whole thing, not rude, just not very warm.

"Look, Clint, if you're not comfortable with this, I can . . ." I can't read the expression on his face so I add, "If you don't want to . . ."

He shakes his head and shrugs. "Why wouldn't I?" *Good question,* I want to say. *Why do I get the feeling that I'm getting the same look from you that you'd give a firing squad?*

"Okay, so here we go, I guess." I pick up my glass and start down the hallway. I can feel Clint right behind me. Steffen or Dave would've had my elbow, but he hasn't made an effort to touch me in any way except to shake my hand.

Oncc we're in the room, he sits down in a chair and I sit on the edge of the bed. "If I understood Dave correctly, your training tonight was supposed to be anal sex."

"That's what he said." There's not a sound in the room. I wait.

"Right then. So any questions before we start?" His gaze is steady. It's like he's looking right through me. I'm not sure he even realizes I'm in the room.

"Yeah. Is this going to hurt?" It's the question that's been burning in my mind.

"Your first time?"

"Yes."

"Then yes, it will. But it's my job to make it bearable and even pleasurable if I can, and to help you know that it will get better if you do it more often." Still no emotion. What is it with this guy?

"So what do I need to do?" It's almost like I'm in a doctor's office, just kind of clinical and cold.

There's something, a shadow of some kind, that passes over his face. "From this point on, that's sir."

"So what do I need to do, Sir?"

"I would appreciate it if you were not so bratty. I won't tolerate that."

That hurts my feelings just a little. "I'm sorry if you thought that's what I was doing, Sir. I wasn't. I was just practicing. I just want to please you, Sir."

He sits there like he's trying to decide if he should stay or run away as fast as he can. Finally, he says, "Remove all of your clothing, sub. Fold it neatly and present yourself to me." I do as I'm told. I really do want to please him. There's something completely unsettling about him, and it's really screwing with my head. I wish I could put a finger on it, but I can't.

When I'm undressed, I present myself to him just as Steffen taught me that first night, and I wait for him to tell me if I've done well, but he doesn't say anything. Then he starts in.

"Anal sex is usually uncomfortable for the bottom at least the first dozen times it's performed. It's important that plenty of lubricant is used, and that the top takes the time to properly prepare the bottom." Originally, I thought he meant "bottom" kind of like "butt," but that must be what I am – a bottom. He's a top. So I understand that. And I feel pretty smart about that, so much so that I must've been smiling to myself, because he stops and says, "What's so funny, sub?"

I put on my best serious expression. "Nothing, Sir. It's just that I understood something you said without asking what it meant, and I was pleased that I did." By the time I finish, I know that what I'm saying doesn't make any sense.

He doesn't seem to care. "Good. Whatever. So it's the top's responsibility to properly prepare you. If ever you're with a top or Dom and you don't think you've been properly prepared, safeword and explain. Otherwise, you could be injured to the point that you'd have to have medical treatment, and no one wants that."

"Good heavens, Sir, no. I certainly wouldn't want that." He makes a "harrumphing" sound until I shudder, and he must realize that I'm sincere.

"No. No one does. If a Dom doesn't properly prepare you, he probably *thinks* he has. Let him know if that's not the case. Now, there are two rings of muscles in the anus, one at the opening . . ." At this point, he goes into a five-minute anatomy litany. I'm not complaining; I learn a lot about the anus during this one. But I'm surprised at how thorough he is. He really is training me, not just doing it to me and hoping that I get it. I'm impressed. When he finishes, I decide a compliment is in order.

"Thank you, Sir. I enjoyed that detailed anatomy lesson."

His face is passive, but he growls, "Impertinence is not appreciated, sub."

I blanch. "I'm sorry, Sir. Please, I'm not being impertinent. I just wanted you to know that I feel much better, much more confident of my safety, because you're so knowledgeable. That's all, Sir. I'm sorry if I came off otherwise, Sir, really. That wasn't my intent." For some reason, I feel tears start to prick my eyes.

For the first time since we came into this room, he reaches over and places his hand on my head. "My only desire is for you to feel safe and satisfied, sub. I'm sorry if I misjudged your comments. Thank you for your confidence in me. I promise I won't let you down." I take a deep breath. *This is going to be okay,* I tell myself.

"Get up on the bed. On your knees, elbows on the mattress. Quickly." I jump up and run to the bed. I try to assume the position, but it's awkward for me. It was easier on the horse that night, but here, the mattress is too soft. Master Clint sees me struggling.

"Sub, hey, it's okay. It's my job to see that everything is as it should be. I can handle your position. Don't worry about it." I hear a snapping sound. "This is lube. It will be cold and it will be messy." It drips down my crack and I'm sure it's falling on the mattress. Plus it's so cold that I shiver a little. I guess my ass wiggles when I do. There's a loud "smack" as his hand comes down on my ass cheek, and I squeal.

"Be still; don't move." I feel a sensation around my tight little hole. His finger? I'm not sure. Then I feel something move into it slowly. It's not very large, so now I'm sure it's his finger. He pumps it in and out a couple of times. Then there's a stretching when he presses what I imagine must be two fingers in there, and I groan.

"Okay? Good to go?" he asks.

I take a deep breath. "Yes, Sir."

"Good." I hear a tearing sound and start to ask, but I realize it's probably a condom wrapper. "Understand that tonight is not about you being satisfied, and it's unlikely that you'd have a climax from first-time anal sex anyway. This is a learning experience. But I will not let you leave here wanting. You will have an orgasm and some kind of satisfaction."

"Yes, Sir."

I feel him climb up onto the bed behind me, and then he grasps my hips with his hands. "I'm going to take it very slow to begin with, but before we're finished, I expect to be fucking into your ass vigorously. It will hurt. I will, however, try to keep it from being excruciating." I feel something against my rosette. "Your safeword?"

"Um, what should it be?" I have no idea what to tell him.

"Most subs use the traffic light approach, red for stop, yellow for slow down and discuss, green for go. Will that work for you?" he asks.

"Sure, Sir. That's easy enough to remember." I'm kind of excited now. I'm about to have an adventure.

That excitement fades pretty quickly. "Oh my god," I whisper as the head of his cock pushes into me. It hurts like a motherfucker. I don't know what to do to make it better.

There's a resounding "crack" as his hand slaps my ass again – hard. He presses in a little, then slaps my ass once more. "Concentrate on the feel of the point of impact of my hand on your skin and try to open up for me. Push from inside. Now take a deep breath. Let it out as I move in, then take in another as I move out. Ready?"

I figure out what he means and in just a few seconds, I feel another burn as the interior ring of muscles is pushed against. When he makes it through that, I cry out. I knew it would hurt, but I didn't know it would hurt this much. "Doing okay?" he asks.

"Yes, Sir," I manage to pant out.

"Color?" he asks. I don't know what he means. "Sub! Your color?"

Oh – the safeword thing. "Um, uh, greenish yellow?"

"Good. I'm about halfway in. Try to relax. I know it's hard, but try." *Yeah, it's hard – you're shoving your cock up my ass. That's hard to relax into.* He presses harder and the burn from my anus is growing wilder. Just when I think I can't take any more, he says, "Very good, sub. I'm all the way in."

I'd like to say there was this enormous feeling of accomplishment, but all I could feel was some measure of relief. I feel him draw out, backing his pelvis away until just the head of his dick is inside me, and then I hear the flip cap on the lube bottle again. "I'm putting more lube on my cock. That will help," he tells me.

When I hear the cap snap again, I know to get ready. Then he says, "Here we go, little one."

He presses straight into me, not a fast, vigorous stroke, but a purposeful, deliberate one. I fight the urge to scream, but before I can settle into it, he pulls back out and shoves back in again. Now I really am burning, but I want to do this, I really want to. Something about him makes me want to please him.

Then he starts a steady rhythm. It isn't fast, but it isn't slow. It's just steady, boring almost all the way into me and then stroking back out before burying his cock in me again. He's been fucking me like this for about three minutes when he says, "Okay, here we go." I shudder and brace myself.

The motion he sets up is almost perpetual. He's moving in and out of me just like anyone would, and three minutes in I realize it doesn't hurt that much anymore. At the seven minute mark, I realize I'm actually kind of enjoying it.

"Sub, your color!" he snaps, and I can tell he's trying to hold back his climax.

"Green, Sir!" I'm almost joyous. I'm getting my ass fucked, and I really kind of like it. Well, more than I thought I would.

And that's when I hear it for the first time: He groans. That sound, the sound of him enjoying my body and getting off in me, sets my entire being on fire, and I feel my skin heat up. I want it, need it, have to have it. He picks up the pace of his pounding into me and I brace myself and take it. His thrusting becomes more frantic, and then suddenly, he stiffens and grips my hips so hard that I'm sure I'll have finger marks. Burying his cock in me as far as he can, he grinds into my ass to relieve the last of his need, and I moan out.

He collects himself somewhat, still buried in my ass. "Sub, your color?"

"Green, Sir. Very, very green." I try not to grin.

"Good." I can't see his face, but he actually sounds pleased. As he pulls out of me he says, "Drop your ass and go into a presentation pose, but keep your torso down." I try to do what he's asking of me and I hear him snap off his condom. Once I'm down like I think he means, he says, "Now, spread your knees apart so your pussy is open." Now I'm face down, resting on my haunches with my knees apart. I feel his hand move between my thighs from behind and then his finger is stroking my clit.

I have trouble sitting still. My hips want to grind, but the way I'm sitting keeps them from being able to move. To insure that, his hand is on my ass, pressing down hard to keep it from coming up at all, and I concentrate on his touch and the heat from his skin on mine. He speeds up his motions and I feel it, the building and gnawing sensation, and then I'm coming, my pussy throbbing and clit pulsing, and I'm trying hard to keep from asking him to stop. And all of a sudden, he does.

His hand strokes down my spine like a breath, and I sigh. "Feel okay?" he asks, his voice quiet.

"Yes, Sir. I do, Sir. Thank you, Sir," I remember to say. That's what I think I'm supposed to say anyway.

"You're welcome. Straighten out and lie down here with me." When I manage to roll onto my side and I'm facing him, I'm surprised to find him lying there looking at me with those deep, dark eyes, waiting for me to cuddle up against him.

I wiggle into his arms, and he wraps them around me. His lips move toward my forehead, and then he stops. It's obvious he's reconsidered the kissing thing. He lifts his head up and back, presses my face into his neck, then drops his chin onto the part in my hair. I lie there for a few minutes, wishing he'd say something to me, taking in his scent. He smells like cinnamon and the smoke from a fireplace, all warm and spicy. Even though I'm sure he doesn't give a whit about me, something in his embrace is comfortable and familiar.

Finally, he says, "That was a good start," and abruptly turns me loose. What the hell? I'm kind of bewildered. I guess he thinks that's enough cuddling.

"I'm sorry, Sir. Did I do something wrong?"

He takes on a sheepish look, and I could almost swear his cheeks are pinking up. "No, no, you did quite well. But I've got to get home. I hope you got something out of this."

"I did. I feel very confident, Sir. Thank you again, Sir." It's very sad. I thought maybe I'd get to know him a little better tonight. I mean, the guy just fucked me in the ass, for god's sake. But he's not going to open up to me at all. I almost think I hear him sigh as he's getting dressed. When he's ready to go, he turns back to me. I'm still on the bed, naked and waiting. I don't know if it's okay for me to get dressed or not.

"Sub, before you go, I want you to pleasure yourself. Then you may get dressed and leave." He doesn't even smile.

"Thank you, Sir," is all I can manage.

To my surprise, he crosses the room and puts his fingers under my chin, lifting my face up to look at him. "You did quite well tonight, Trish. You're going to make a good sub for some lucky Dom someday, I can tell." With that, he turns and strides out of the room.

I slip my hand down between my legs and start to stroke my over-sensitized nub. It only takes me a few minutes to come, his face in my memory, and then I'm ready to leave. As I dress, I see something on the floor.

It's a business card – Clint's business card. He must've dropped it. The face of the card is a deep green, almost black, and in gold letters are the words, "Clinton Alexander Winstead, Corporate Training and Efficiency Consultant. Reasonable Hourly Rates. Specializing in the Small Business Community." So that's what he does for a living – he's a consultant. I realize the only place I have to keep the card is in my bra, so that's where it goes for the time being.

When I get back to the bar, Clint's nowhere in sight, but Dave's back. "What in the hell did you do to him in there?" he asks me, a weird look in his eyes.

I scrunch my face up and raise one eyebrow. "What do you mean?" To my knowledge, I didn't do a damn thing to him.

"Something happened. He was almost running when he came back out here and barely spoke, just went rushing out the door."

I shrug. "I didn't do anything, I don't think." Before I can stop myself, I blurt out, "He's a strange one."

"Not strange," Dave says quietly, and almost so low that I can't hear him, he adds, "He's just got a lot of hurt."

"Are you ever going to tell me what that means?" My frustration is mounting.

"Nope." Dave starts wiping down the bar. "Eventually he'll have to tell you himself."

My training is going pretty well, I think. At least Dave says it is. I've done all kinds of things I never thought I would do, but I haven't had sex out in the public areas with anyone yet. I'm not sure I can do that.

The part I liked best was the bondage and restraint. I know that sounds awful, but I find it kind of soothing. It's like being told, "You will like this or else," and then being shown that it's true.

My favorite is the spreader bar. I can't back out with it, because I can't get my knees together. I like all of the cuffs and straps and things like that. I *don't* like the gags – at all. Dave knows it so he makes me wear one almost every night. I dread that; I'm not a fan of drool and I'm afraid of choking. But so far, so good.

We've been working, or playing rather, four nights a week for two months. Dave surprises me tonight. "Baby, I think I need to cut you loose."

"Huh? What?" I'm not sure what he means.

"You're ready." He smiles at me, and I can't help but think how gorgeous he is. Having sex with him has been, well, quite the adventure in itself. "I think you could handle anything a Dom could throw at you and probably come back for more. So I think you're graduating from 'The Uncle Dave School for Wayward Submissives.' Congratulations!" He sets a cosmo down in front of me, and I grin back at him.

"Are you sure about this?" I don't *feel* ready, whatever that means.

"Yep. And it's a good thing too. There's an event coming up pretty soon, and I want you to participate if you can. Got any vacation time?"

"Actually, I don't have a job right now." Dave looks alarmed. "I quit yesterday. They were working me to death. Don't worry, though. I had six weeks of vacation time coming to me and I'm bleeding Ron's bank accounts, so I have some money. I'll have to get a job pretty soon, but right now, I'm good." I take another sip. "So what's this event?"

"It's the annual 'try before you buy' event. Some of the guys laugh and call it 'The Sub Club.' It's actually called 'The Pairing.' We pair up Doms and subs and they cohabitate and play together for two weeks. Then, two weeks after everyone has split up, we have a night when Doms can come in and offer to collar subs. We've had some really good pairings come out of it."

"Oh, no, that . . . I-I-I don't think I could do that," I stutter. What the hell? With my luck I'd get paired with some axe murderer, but then I remember that Dave is involved, so it should be okay. He won't let that happen, at least not if he knows. That realization lets my curiosity kick back in. "So exactly what does this entail?"

He laughs. "I knew that curiosity of yours would get the better of you!" I find it more than a little disconcerting that he can almost read my mind. He spends the next forty-five minutes explaining to me how it all works. Then he asks the big question: "Is there a Dom here you think you'd like to be collared by?"

Dozens of faces spin, and then they line up like cherries in a slot machine. Clint. Oh, no – that's no good. I try again and get Steffen. Now *that* might work out okay. "Um, maybe Steffen? We've played together a few times and I like him well enough. I don't know enough about him to make that kind of decision, though."

"That's the idea of the two weeks. But you might not get Steffen. You need to be open to whomever the pairing puts you with. It's drawn randomly, so there's no way of knowing."

I shudder. Two weeks alone with a guy I don't even know, having sex and doing god only knows what else. That sounds like . . . fun. At least it could be.

Chapter 4

It's the night of the event. For the first time ever, I go out into the big room naked from the waist up. At first I feel kind of shaky and conspicuous, but then I notice that no one is just standing around open-mouthed staring at me, so it's okay.

There are Doms and subs *everywhere*. The place is elbow to elbow. There must be three hundred people here, and I wonder what the fire marshal would say if he could see this. Some are guys I haven't noticed around here before, but they're bound to be members or they wouldn't be allowed in. Most of them are regulars, though, and that makes me feel a little better. There are some lady Dommes too. Dave calls out for everyone to put their cards in the bins so the sorting can begin, Doms in one, subs in the other. There are different sets of bins depending on what members are looking for. There are Doms who want a male sub, lady Dommes who want a lady sub, male subs who want a lady Domme, all kinds of combinations.

The drawing begins. One particularly nasty-looking Dom gets a beautiful young sub. She looks like she's scared to death. Then Arlo, who's a total goofball, gets one of the older women as his sub; I don't know how she'll stand him for two weeks.

The most interesting one is a sub named Vance. He showed up at the club in pigtails, a big cowboy hat, snip-toe cowboy boots, leather chaps, and a pair of black bikini briefs that read "Here's The Beef" in yellow letters across the ass. He's eyeing a Domme who's about six two and weighs probably three hundred pounds. She's wearing a skin-tight leather bodysuit, thigh-high leather stiletto-heeled boots, a wide leather belt with a huge silver buckle, and a ponytail on top of her head wrapped with silver chain. And she's carrying a bullwhip woven in black and purple leather. When she looks his way, he dances from foot to foot like he's the most excited guy in the whole world.

About halfway through, it happens: "Patricia Stinson." So nervous I can barely stand, I make my way to the stage. Once I'm there, Dave draws out the Dom card and I want to crawl under a chair.

"Clint Winstead."

I halfway expect him to come to the stage, say he won't take me because he hates me, and then stomp away. What the hell will I do if that happens? I see him making his way through the crowd and he finally reaches the stage. I look over at him, terrified; he doesn't smile.

"Master Clint Winstead, do you accept the pairing?" I'm pretty sure I'm about to break out in hives.

"Yes, Dungeon Master, I accept the pairing."

For a split second I thought I'd misunderstood. I look over at Clint, who growls at me, "Sub, eyes averted." Shit. He's getting started right now. I thought I'd be happy if he accepted me for pairing, even daydreamed about it a little, but now I'm not so sure this is a good idea. Two weeks with a guy who can't stand me is going to be brutal. Why would he say yes?

He motions me down off the stage and I follow him at a respectful distance as I've been taught. When we get to the back hallway he turns and says, "Get your things so we can go and get started." I don't say a word, just walk into the locker room, get my stuff, and head back out. He's waiting for me in the hallway, and I follow him out of the building. No one pays any attention to us; they're waiting for the rest of the pairings to be announced.

When we reach his car, he surprises me – he opens the door for me in a very chivalrous manner and takes my arm to help me in. I realize that, even though he doesn't seem to like me, he's always been polite to me. That makes me feel a little better.

"Have you eaten?" he asks once he's in.

"No." He shoots me a look. "Oh, sorry. Sir." I give him a little smile but he doesn't smile back. "I was too nervous." He looks like he's about to ask me something, but changes his mind.

The adventure is about to begin, but I've got a feeling the fun is at an end. Yup – it's gonna be a long two weeks.

We stop and have a burger on our way to Clint's; he barely speaks to me while we're eating. I'd already packed some things, so I didn't have to stop at home. When we pull up to his house, I'm surprised. It's just a normal, modest-looking house. I don't know what I was expecting. A house of horrors, maybe? Like the Bates Motel? Who knows?

I open the car door but before I can get out, he's there. As soon as I stand up, he says, "From this point on, you will allow me to assist you with doors, chairs, all of those kinds of things. It's a sign of my respect for you." That one surprises me. "As long as we're outside the house in the vanilla world, we'll act vanilla – with a few exceptions. Once inside, it's my rules."

He opens the door and motions for me to pass him and go inside, then turns on the light. It's a nice house, nice furnishings, kind of warm and homey. I think I was expecting industrial steel and vinyl and spotlights, with eye bolts on every surface. Not like that at all. Then he gives me the grand tour. "Living room, kitchen," he points, "and the laundry room is back there." Down the hallway we go. "My bedroom and bath." Two of the doors are closed; he doesn't open them, but he points to one and says, "Home office." At the end of the hall he opens a door and points in. "Your room."

I have my own room. Now I'm confused. In answer to my unspoken question, he says, "Sometimes you will be in my bed. But not always. And if things get too intense, this gives you a sanctuary to quiet your mind and rest, somewhere to retreat to."

I whisper, "Thank you, Sir." Once I've dropped my bag on the bed, I follow him back into the living area.

He motions for me to take a seat on the sofa, and I remember I don't have panties on. I look at the cushions and he says, "Oh. Sorry." He disappears for a few seconds and comes back with a bath towel, which he spreads out on the sofa. Then he motions for me to sit again, and I try to be graceful as I do.

"Protocol. I am the master of this house. It's literally my way or the highway here. You are the sub. You are not a slave. You are not expected to do all of the housework, but I would appreciate it if you did some."

"I won't mind at all, Sir."

"Good. You will be nude at all times inside the house unless I specify otherwise, or unless you're performing a task that would be dangerous to your skin. Your only articles of clothing will be a training collar and the heels I give you. Size seven and a half?"

I gasp. "How did you know that, Sir?"

"Good guess." He stops, then starts again. "You will wear the training collar for as long as you're here. That will make restraining you easier in a jam." What kind of jam would make me need to be restrained? I don't really understand that, but I nod. "You will meet me at the door when I come in. I expect you to be nude and in the collar and heels, kneeling at the door in presentation. Be aware that I may fuck you immediately upon returning home."

"Yes, Sir."

"I am not a sadist, but I do enjoy bondage, restraints, and discipline sessions with my subs. This is only for the purpose of arousal. I will, however, punish if needed for an infraction. Discipline and punishment are very different. You'll learn the difference. But know this: Sex will never be used to punish. Never. I don't believe in that. And I think the punishment should fit the crime. With that in mind, a word of warning: I can be very creative in my punishment methods, so be afraid." He doesn't crack a smile, and I swallow hard.

"You will sleep in your room unless I tell you to stay in my bed. If I want, I will chain you to the bed so you cannot get out unless I give you permission. But if you're in my bed, you always need permission to get out. Bathroom, drink of water, doesn't matter. Permission required. And no closed doors. You will shower, shave, toilet, everything with the door open."

I nod. This doesn't seem too bad, just the usual dominance stuff. "While you are here, your sex belongs to me. All of it. You will not have sex with anyone else if we go to the club unless I tell you to, and if I tell you to, you will do so. You will not touch yourself in such a way as to arouse yourself or satisfy yourself unless I so direct. Your body, your arousal, your orgasms, they all belong to me. Is that understood?" I nod again. "Good. There will be times when I leave you wanting and unsatisfied for an extended period of time. I do practice forced orgasm and orgasm denial as discipline, and you are not to pleasure yourself unless I give express permission, and that's usually for my entertainment. Do you understand?"

"Yes, Sir," I whisper.

"Good. The two doors that are closed in the hallway are off limits to you. One is the office. The other," he stops, then starts again, "is my kids' bedroom."

"You have children, Sir?" I had no idea.

"Yes. Two girls, ages ten and eight. You will not meet them. They're with my mother." *Okay then, good enough to fuck but not good enough to meet your kids. I get it*, I think. "I was once married. I do not want to talk about it, so do not ask. If you forget and ask, that will be okay the first time. The second time you will be punished." Wow. He doesn't intend to share anything about himself with me. I get that now too. "I understand that you were married. That's all I need to know. I don't need details. I'm really not interested." Ouch.

"Yes, Sir."

"Any questions?"

"Yes, Sir. What do I do if I'm alone here and the doorbell or the phone rings? Do I answer it?"

"Do not answer the door. Please do answer the phone and take a message for me. Most of my calls come in on my cell, though, so there shouldn't be too many instances of that. Anything else?"

"I don't think so, Sir." At least I've stopped shaking, but that's about it. "And may I call you Master, Sir?"

"Interchangeably. Sir or Master. Makes no difference to me as long as you show me the respect I deserve as your Dominant."

"Yes, Sir. Absolutely."

"Then go and put your things away. Sometime in the next couple of days we'll go and get more of your things. But you won't need many clothes." Yeah, I get that too. "You'll find your collar and heels in the closet. When you have them on, come back out here and kneel in front of the sofa." He turns and strolls into the kitchen. I assume that means I've been dismissed, so I go back to the bedroom.

Sure enough, the heels and collar are in the closet, the heels on a shelf and the collar on a hook. It's obvious the collar's been worn before; it's obvious the heels are brand new. I try them on and they fit perfectly except they're five-inch stilettos and I don't wear heels, especially not heels that high. I'll probably fall and kill myself, but I'll wear them until the coroner gets here.

When I'm undressed and wearing the collar and shoes, I go back out and kneel in front of the sofa. It feels like I'm there forever and there's no sign of him. Just when I think I misunderstood, I hear footsteps and look up just in time to see him come out of the hallway.

He's naked – gloriously, beautifully naked. The night he did my anal workout he was behind me the whole time, and he never completely undressed. This is something else entirely. I'm trying not to stare, but it's hard. I mean, literally, it's hard. Big and hard. And his body is amazing, the epitome of the perfect male specimen, a smattering of dark hair across his pecs drifting inward and downward, ending at his beautiful cock. I think I must've let out a gasp or something because he asks, "Sub, is there something you want to say?"

Now I'm embarrassed. "No, Sir."

He stands for a few seconds and waits, but I don't elaborate. Finally, he says, "Stand. Back to me. Feet spread, hands on the sofa." I go through everything he just said and realize that the heels put me at just the right height for him to come up behind me.

But he surprises me when he sits down on the floor, then scoots under me and turns around. His back is against the front of the sofa, and his face is . . . oh, my god. "Put your hands on my shoulders," he demands. His fingers draw my pussy lips apart and he can see it all, touch it all, and I feel myself go wet. I feel his hands go up my groin, up my belly, up my lower ribs, and suddenly clutch my breasts, the thumb and index finger of each hand twisting my already-erect peaks. After he's twisted and pulled them for a good three minutes, his hands wander back down my body and spread my slit open again.

"Wet and ready. Your cunt is very pretty when it's engorged and hot. And it smells delicious." I was worried that I hadn't had time to sort of clean up. Guess that's not an issue. "You will hold still and you will remain silent. Not a peep or a groan. Do you understand?"

"Yes, Sir." Then I wonder, *Was I supposed to answer him out loud?*

Before I can ask, I feel his tongue slide up into my slit, and the tip enters my pussy. It's velvety and hot, and then he drags it upward to my hard little pearl. The miracle that is his mouth engulfs my dripping sex and laps at it, and I have to work to keep a moan in. When he circles my clit with his tongue, I can barely stand. I think my legs might give out, but he's holding me steady.

Just when I think it can't get any wilder, he sucks my nub in between his lips and I feel faint. He's working it in and out of those hot lips, and then he scrapes it with his teeth. I almost scream. He starts with the tongue circling again, and I'm struggling to be still and quiet, but it's almost impossible. About the time I've got it under control again, he wraps his hands around my hips and then slaps my ass – hard.

My body gives in and I shudder with my release. I can feel my hips start to churn, but I can't get away from his mouth with him holding my hips that way, and staying quiet takes everything I've got. The orgasm goes on and on, and I'm biting my tongue to keep from crying out. I feel my knees give way, but I guess he anticipated it because he catches me and lowers me.

But when he lowers me, it's straight down, and he impales me on his long, thick, hard shaft. I almost gasp. "Wrap your legs around behind me. Go ahead and kick the heels off. You won't need them right now." When my legs are around him, he says, "You don't have to do anything. I'll do all the work. Just feel me inside you, stroking you, filling you. Am I stretching you, sub? You may speak."

"Yes, Sir," I manage to pant out. He's hitting just the right spot and my vision is starting to blur.

"Good. Will you come for me?" His lifting and dropping of me picks up speed, and everything below my waist tenses. Watching his biceps as he moves me up and down on his length makes me burn all over.

"Yes, Sir. I want to come for you, Sir." It's building, and fast. I feel the ache inside me and I'm awash with longing, my clit dragging down his pelvis, his hands under my ass, lifting and dropping me, my arms around his neck, helping even though he said I didn't have to. The need is so strong that I feel like I'm losing myself in it, dropping down into it, being swallowed up by it. "Oh, god, Sir, I want to come for you, Sir." Time is slowing down and everything in my body is swelling, expanding, trembling. This room, his body, my thirst for him, they're all that's left in the whole world.

"Then come for me, sub. Let go for me," he growls and bites my shoulder. No one's ever done that to me before, and it feels like a lit match to a powder keg. My insides explode, shatter, start to spasm and throb, and my body falls into the climax like a skydiver out of an airplane. I cry out over and over, but even in my ecstasy I feel his cock start to pulse inside me and his hot, bitter syrup fills me to bursting.

He lets me fall onto his shaft, its length and girth embedded solidly in me, and drop to his chest, my arms around his neck. His hands slide from my ass up around my waist and grip me to him. I'm drifting along, floating on a breeze, feeling light and free, and then his finger under my chin tips my face up and he kisses me.

It's a long, scorching kiss, his tongue forcing my mouth open and lashing against mine. I moan through his lips and return the desperation, latching onto him and refusing to let go. The kiss goes on and on, like it's binding us together, making us one. When he finally releases me, he pushes me back so he can look into my face. "Look into my eyes, sub," he whispers.

When I look up, his eyes lock onto mine and I suddenly feel naked and embarrassed. The raw sexuality in those dark pools snatches my breath away. "Are you satisfied?" he asks. My mind screams, *Really? You have to ask me that?*

"Yes, Sir, totally." With a hand on the back of my neck, he draws my face to his shoulder and hugs me against him, holding me there while he goes soft inside me. "Are you satisfied, Sir?"

"For now. I will be using you like this often during the day. When you leave in two weeks, you will have been fucked more than you have been in your whole life previously. I will fuck you everywhere in this house, in every way I can think of and some I'll probably invent. Is that something you want?"

I shiver all over. "Oh, yes, Sir. Absolutely."

"Good." He pushes me back again to look at me. "Go to your bathroom and clean yourself up, then go to bed. Set your alarm for six o'clock in the morning, get up and go to the bathroom to relieve yourself and freshen up, then come to my bed. Be prepared to please me immediately upon your arrival. Is that clear?"

"Yes, Sir. Thank you, Sir."

He helps me up and stands beside me. I reach down and pick up my shoes, but he says, "No. You will put them on and wear them. I want to watch you walk down the hall with my cum running down your legs." I do exactly as he says, and I can feel his eyes on me as I walk down the hall, trying to do so in the sexiest way I can manage, considering I'm not used to heels. And I do feel his cum trickle down my legs, a hot river of sex rolling down my skin.

The one thing I noticed throughout the whole encounter is that he didn't smile one single time. Matter of fact, I can't remember ever seeing him look anything but serious. And that becomes my mission.

I want to see Clint Winstead smile.

I'm settled between his legs, face down, mouth over his cock. It was raging and purple when I came in, and now it's huge and swollen in my throat. As I lick, suck, and take it all in, he talks to me like I'm in a job interview.

"You did a decent job of coming when I told you to last night. Before you leave here I'm hoping to have you trained so that you come when I tell you to, every time I tell you to." He stops for a second and I can feel him watching me. "A little less tongue, a lot more sucking. As I was saying, you will come when I tell you to. I will say, you did look beautiful riding me. Your pussy is lovely to look at and feels good, plenty tight enough. You show a lot of promise." I moan around his cock. "You're welcome." I stifle a giggle.

In just a couple of minutes he cries out, "Oh, yeah, drink me down," and shoots a load and a half down my throat. He holds my head down over him for maybe twenty seconds, then pulls it up and says, "Look up at me, sub." When my eyes meet his, he says, "Your lips look good around my shaft. Very nice job. We'll do it again in a few hours. Turn around, knees and elbows."

Once I'm in position, I hear him snap on a condom and then I feel lube dripping down my crack and a finger in my ass. Within minutes, his dick is buried in my tight little hole, dragging in and out, and I cry out as the friction lights my internal fire.

"Don't just make noise, sub. Tell me what you want."

"I want you to fuck me, Sir!"

"How? Do you want it in the ass? Do you want it hard?"

"Yes, Sir! Hard and in my ass, Sir! Please, please, Sir!" I'm panting now, needing it so bad that I can barely think or speak. His fingers are digging into my hips as he holds them and pulls me back onto his rigidness, plunging forward into me. I feel his cock plump up and then he's emptying his balls into the condom, grinding against my ass and groaning.

But before I can say anything, he flips me over onto my back and has a pair of cuffs on me in a flash. Just as I realize what he's done, he secures them to the headboard with a chain, then orders, "Open your legs! Show me your cunt!"

I do exactly that, and he begins to stroke my clit, roughly and fairly fast, and I almost scream with desire. The ass fucking prepped me for this, and I need it, want it, am begging for it. "Oh, god, Sir, make me come! Please make me come!" I feel the slow simmer start behind my swollen bud and my hips start to rock, waiting for the rolling boil. And just as I feel it starting to consume me . . .

He stops.

I cry out, "Oh, god, Sir! Please!"

"Look at me, sub!" he orders. I look up into his eyes and see their darkness piercing into mine. He draws my slit open and looks at my clit. "Huge. Swollen. Red. Needy. And for now it'll stay that way."

"Oh, god, Sir, please, don't leave me like this, please!" I cry out.

He reaches up and takes my chin in his hand. "If you had any doubts before, perhaps this will drive home the point. Any brattiness, any disobedience, any flaw that your service could have, understand that I will fuck it right out of you in the next two weeks." He leans down over me so that his mouth is against my ear and whispers, "For the next two weeks, you and your swollen cunt will be my fuck. You'll savor so much of my cum that you'll want it in your coffee, dripped into your tea, stirred into those damn cosmos you love so much." Now I'm so aroused that I feel like I'll faint. "My spluge will be in every hole in your body and it will start to feel like second nature to be filled with it. Ever wonder what it would be like to live with a cock stuffed into you all day every day?" I nod and whimper. "Well, you're going to get a chance to find out."

Chapter 5

By eleven o'clock I've lost count of how many times he's fucked me. And he hasn't let me come once. I'm in misery.

I'm still chained to the head of the bed when he straddles my torso. "Now I'll get you ready to go to the store." He grabs the bottle of lube, pours a generous amount between my breasts, and presses them together. I'm pretty sure I know where this is going, and I'm right – he traps his dick between them and begins to thrust.

I lie there, watching his cock head popping in and out of my cleavage, and I see him stiffen. When he comes, he throws a ropy stream of semen onto my chest. And he starts again immediately.

I've never seen a man come as many times as he has. And he's never soft, always hard. I want to ask him if he takes one of those erectile dysfunction pills, but I don't think so. It seems his body is just so well-trained that he can stay hard. It's pretty amazing, actually, after old one-and-done Ron.

He comes two more times on my chest. To my surprise, he releases my hands, but he's still sitting on my ribcage. When the cuffs are off my wrists, he says, "Use your hands to decorate your body with my cum."

I start smearing it around on me. "Up your chest, across to your shoulders, all over the tops of your breasts. Put it on your nipples too. Yeah, just like that. Very pretty." He looks down to admire his handiwork, then gets up and pulls me to a sitting position.

"May I wash my hands, Sir?" I ask, showing him my palms.

"Oh, no. I want all of this to dry on you." He goes to the drawers where I've put my clothes and pulls out a short skirt and a tee. "Put these on. No panties, no bra. Flip-flops. We're going to the store. Let it dry and, when you're dressed, kneel in the living room."

With his cum all over me? I'm more than horrified. This qualifies as humiliation. As soon as it's dry, I pull on the clothes, then go to the living room. I've still got cum all over my hands, so I'm afraid to touch anything. When he comes into the room, he looks down at me. "So rise and follow me to the car." I do exactly as he says. Once in the car, he fastens my seatbelt buckle so I don't get ejac all over it.

He goes to a part of town where I've never been before. It's not close to his house *or* my house. I don't know anything about this area of town. We pull up in the parking lot, but instead of letting me out, he says, "Pull up your shirt."

"Here, Sir?" I can't believe he wants me to do this in the parking lot.

"Yes. Right now. Pull it up." He reaches into his pocket and pulls something out, then leans over and starts to suck and chew on my left nipple. When it's hard and tight, he puts the nozzle of a bulb over it, sucks my nipple into the bulb, and slides a rubber ring off the bulb's tip and onto my nipple. It traps the blood there, so it immediately begins to throb, sending jolts of white-hot need straight to my clit. Then he does the same with the other one. I guess to myself that I'm going to be left in the car.

But he comes around and opens my door. When I sit and stare at him, he says, "Oh. Sorry," and reaches in to undo my seatbelt. "Now pull your shirt down and come on. We only have about fifteen minutes before those have to come off. I'd hate to have to do that in the middle of the store."

I know everyone in the store is staring at me and my huge, hard nipples sticking right straight out. Because it's a tee that I'm wearing, they're poking out obscenely. We walk through the store, getting funny looks from everyone coming toward us.

When we get into the produce department, I see an employee eyeing me. Finally, he comes toward us and I'm sure he's going to ask us to leave.

Instead, he walks up, looks at Clint, and says, "I've been watching your girl here. Impressive. Want to make a trade?"

"Sure. What've you got?"

"I'd love to fuck her. Want your groceries free?"

For the first time, Clint almost grins. "Sure. That sounds like a great swap. Let's go back into the office. I want to watch."

I can't believe my ears. He wants this guy to fuck me? He wants to *watch* this guy fuck me? We head off down the little hallway, go into the office, and he closes the door. "Shirt off. Pull your skirt up around your waist," Clint growls at me, and I do as he says. "And you're not allowed to come, sub." I just *knew* he was going to say that.

The grocery guy says, "Put one foot on the desk." When I do, my whole snatch is exposed, downright gaping open. The guy pulls out his cock, walks up, and starts to fuck me. While he's stroking into me, he's twisting and pulling my purple nipples. The pain is excruciating and horribly, terribly, unbelievably arousing. I'm also a little afraid; Clint didn't make him wear a condom, and that scares me, but the fear is exciting too. Out of the corner of my eye, I see Clint pull out his cock and start to stroke himself. I'm so embarrassed that I can barely breathe and so turned on that I can barely stand still.

But in that moment I realize that I'm standing in a business office, nude, satisfying two men at once, one of them a guy I don't even know who's fucking away in me like there's no tomorrow. There must be something wrong with me, because I feel some kind of elation, like I'm a newly-born sex goddess or a porn star. The guy is grinding into me and I feel his release; there is absolutely no concern or consideration for my satisfaction, none. At about the same time, Clint lets loose and shoots a spurt of cum into the air.

"You can take your foot down now and get dressed," the grocery guy says. He pulls his dick back into his pants and turns to Clint. "Nice fuck, man. I like the way you barter. Groceries are on the house."

"Thanks, man. Glad you enjoyed her. Great trade. Heading for the checkout."

"No problem. Come back anytime. Really! And by the way, love those nipples. I bet they hurt, don't they, sweet pussy?"

Without meeting his eyes, I say, "Yes, Sir. They hurt very good, Sir."

"Nice! Hope I get to fuck you again sometime." He opens the door and Clint motions for me to go out. Once back out in the store, he gathers all of the things we were supposed to be getting, then makes me stand with him at the checkout, the grocery guy's cum running down the inside of my thighs and my hard, rigid nipples poking out under my tee. I'm ever so thankful when the man comes and signs off on our receipt.

Clint stows the groceries in the trunk, then helps me into the car and gets in on his side. "Shirt up," he growls. I lift it and look; my nipples are dark purple and throbbing. He grabs them and twists and pulls them one more time, and I pray that he'll stroke me until I orgasm. Instead, he says, "Gotta take these off now." He puts his mouth over one and I feel him drawing the little ring off with his teeth. When it pops off, the blood rushes in and

I almost shriek. He performs the same ritual with the other one. By that time, I'm panting.

We pull out of the parking lot and head back to the house. I'm still trying to understand what just happened. He traded me for a couple of bags of groceries. I don't know how I'm supposed to feel about that.

Once the groceries are put away, he says, "Undress and kneel in front of the sofa." I do so immediately and wait, sticky all over from the cum on my chest and down my legs. I've done it – I've followed his instructions to the letter, and I'm sure he's going to tell me how pleased he is with me. When he comes into the living room, he sits down on the sofa and says, "Turn toward me. Eyes on mine." I turn and face him, looking straight into his eyes. And he shocks the shit out of me with what he says.

"Trish, listen to me. That guy I just let fuck you? He's a Dom from the club. I pre-arranged all of that." I gasp. His face goes somber, as somber as I've seen it. "I want you to remember that I said this: If any Dom ever tries to trade sex with you for anything, groceries, clothes, drugs, alcohol, smokes, a car, anything, get the hell out. That would be the epitome of disrespect, and you don't have to subject yourself to that. No Dom should *ever* ask you to compromise yourself that way. Do you understand me?"

I swallow hard. He was trying to teach me something, and it worked. "Yes, Sir. I won't ever let anyone do that to me again, Sir." There are tears in my eyes and

I feel so foolish and dirty. "I was just trying to please you, Sir."

"And if that had really been a stranger, you could've been hurt badly. I do appreciate your trust in me, though, but don't do it with anyone else – ever. Please?"

Even though I'm trying not to, a tear escapes my eye and rolls down my cheek. "No, Sir, I won't."

He puts his fingers under my chin and pulls my face up to look into it. "I hope this taught you something. You need to value yourself. No matter how your own Dom uses you, he has your best interests at heart. But someone who would do that to you is not worthy of your service or loyalty. Never forget that." I try to smile my tears away and, to my surprise, he leans down and kisses my forehead. "Get in the shower. By the way, his name is Gary and he's a really good guy. He said he thinks the next time he has a new sub he'll ask me to do the same thing with her so she gets a lesson that will stick. Now go get cleaned up."

I rise and head down the hall, still in a state of disbelief. If he was looking to make an impression on me, it didn't just work – it's indelible.

The hot water feels good on my skin, but I'm still in need. I've been fucked so many times already that I can't count them and I still haven't been allowed to come. As I wash myself, I start to take a few extra passes with the washcloth. Before too long, I feel an orgasm coming on, and I look toward the hallway. Clint's nowhere to be found, so I go ahead and satisfy myself, careful not to make a sound.

Once I'm showered and dried off, I wobble back out to the living room on my stilettos and kneel in front of the sofa. I have no idea where Clint is, so I just wait. In a few minutes he appears in the kitchen doorway and motions for me to come to him.

I rise and stroll into the kitchen, if you could call it strolling. There, on a chair, is a strange-looking, rectangular thing covered in bristles and, whatever it is, it's still got the tag on it. "I guess you're wondering what that is?" he asks.

"Yes, Sir. It's weird, Sir. I've never seen one of those before."

"It's a shoe cleaner. You put it on the ground, stand on it with one foot, and brush the other foot back and forth in it to get the mud off your shoe, then reverse." He stands and seems to be admiring it. "Guess you're wondering what it's doing there?"

"The thought had crossed my mind, Sir." I get the feeling I'm not going to like this.

"You're going to sit on it." He points at it. "Spread your pussy lips apart and sit down with the center ridge right down the middle of your slit."

At first I think he's kidding, but then I realize he's serious. There's a raised row of bristles that look like wooden splinters right down the middle of this thing, and when I sit down, the lips of my cunt fall on either side of the bristled ridge and the bristles poke straight into my lady bits. It's wildly uncomfortable. I try not to wriggle and squirm too much, because the more I move, the worse it starts to hurt.

I'm blinking back tears when he says, "I told you that your sex belongs to me. And you defied me in the shower." How in the hell did he know? I'm mortified. "This is your punishment. You will sit here until I tell you that you can get up." He sets the timer on his phone, but for how long I have no idea.

The more I settle into it, the more it hurts. Plus, with the height of the chair, it's impossible to use my feet and legs to hover over it. Sitting on it is all I can do. With every second that passes it's more painful. I can see the kitchen clock and I watch five, ten, fifteen, twenty minutes pass. At twenty-five I start to get really panicky. At thirty he says, "That's enough. Would you like to go back to the shower and pleasure yourself right now?"

"No, Sir, no way," I say, eyes on the floor.

"Good. I'm going to fuck your sore pussy. This is neither punishment nor discipline; this is a Dom using his sub as he sees fit. Reach down and grab your ankles." When I do so, he backs me up against a wall and, quick as lightning, his prick is buried in my sheath. He pounds me so hard that my back is banging against the wall. After he's come, he says, "Stand there just like that. I'll tell you when you can straighten up." I know it's another ten minutes before he finally says, "Stand."

I'm stiff. I'm also dizzy from having my head down for so long, and he takes my arm until I get my equilibrium back. "Do not defy me again. I always know." I believe him.

"No, Sir. I will not."

"Good." He points down the hallway. "Go and rest for about fifteen minutes. I'll probably fuck you again after that."

"Yes, Sir. Thank you for the lessons, Sir, and for fucking me, Sir," I murmur. As I walk, I fight a grin because the sluttiest thought is going through my head: *I don't want to lie down. I want to fuck you again, Sir. I want you to fuck me until my pussy is broken.* I figure that would take forever, and that's exactly how long I want him pounding into me.

We're together in his big bed. Instead of something vigorous, this seems more like lovemaking. On our sides, we rock against each other until we climax, then start again. It's more like a beautiful ballet than fucking. Everywhere he touches me, I can almost feel his fingerprints being etched into my skin, and it gives me a thrill I've never felt before. I thought Dave was gorgeous, but Clint is something entirely different, chiseled features but not harsh, hair short and sexy but just long enough that the curl is obvious, muscled up but not muscle-bound. He's a man, all man, sweetness and hard-edged passion, with the seriousness of an old soul. I know that somewhere in that super-heated, lust-driven package there's got to be the playfulness of a child. I hope I can find it.

He looks into my face with something that passes for tenderness. "I've got to come up with a name for you. I can't just keep calling you sub." He looks thoughtful for a minute, then says, "Would you like for me to call you Vännan?"

"What does that mean, Sir?" I ask, kissing the side of his neck. He responds by nipping my earlobe.

"It's Swedish for 'lover.'" He pulls my face to his and kisses me long and deep. I melt into him and kiss him back.

"Have you ever given it to another sub?" I have to ask; I can't stand not knowing if this is his standard sub name.

He shakes his head, his eyes closed. "No. It will be yours if you want it."

"It's beautiful, Sir. I'd like that very much."

He takes one of my hands and kisses the back of it. "Then Vännan it is."

Vännan. Lover. It's precious. And so is he. I just wish I could tell him how precious he is. I'm sure he has no idea.

I call Sheila and tell her where I am and what's going on. Since I haven't shared anything with her before, I think it's about time.

"You're doing what? With whom?" she screams. "Are you kidding?"

"No! You should see him. He's gorgeous." He's gone to the dry cleaner's to pick up some suits. I asked him if it was okay for me to call Sheila, and he told me to feel free. But he also told me to finger myself, take a picture, and text it to him while he was gone. So I'm talking to her on speaker and trying not to pant while I follow his instructions. I send the photo and get a text back:

Nice. But a little more to the left. LOL JK

"But I don't understand. Is he spanking you?"

I start to laugh. "Only if my behavior warrants. I have rules to follow. I get punished if I break them. And I get rewarded if I obey. Richly rewarded. I mean hugely richly. Enormously."

She giggles. "I get it, I get it! He's hung." I giggle like I'm fourteen. "Do I get to meet this guy?"

My stomach knots. "I doubt it. It's only for two weeks." *He's given me a pet name when I'm only staying for two weeks.* I find that kind of confusing, but I'll take what I can get.

"Oh. Well, I guess you should have fun while you can, huh?" Sheila sounds kind of down. "Just take care of yourself, okay? This all happened because of that incredible older guy at the bar that night?"

"Yeah. And he's the best, Sheila. Dave has turned into a really good friend."

I hear a sadness in her voice when she says, "I hope you won't forget about your old friends."

"Never, sister. Never."

I think things are going pretty well. He's hot and cold, and I hate that, but so far things are pretty good.

Sometimes he fucks me fast and hard, over and over, while I beg for more. Sometimes we rock together like we've always known each other, a sweet thing while it lasts. I'm never really sure what's going to happen next, but I'm pretty sure it's going to be amazing. At least the sex.

On Wednesday he announces, "We're going to the club tonight. I'll pick out something for you to wear. Go shower." When I get out of the shower, a pair of black stretch short-shorts and black seamed stockings are lying on the bed with a pair of black stilettos on the floor. The top he's put out for me is more or less a bra, and it has little slits up the middle of the cups with ribbon tie closures. In other words, if they're untied, my nipples will be completely exposed. That's intriguing.

I was hoping he'd give me a prettier collar to wear when we go out, but he doesn't, just the training collar. Once he's helped me buckle it on, we go to the door, where he gives me the once-over and says, "Mmmm-mmmm-mmmm; you're a scrumptious kind of fuckable. Remember, eyes averted and no talking to other Doms." I nod. With that, we head out and make it to the club just as it's opening.

There's already a crowd milling about. He retrieves two drinks from the bar – Dave's nowhere in sight – and we head over to watch the scenes. Clint brought a leash and snapped it onto my collar. He says it's not to lead me, but rather to keep other Doms away. Looks like it's working pretty well. No one will even look at me.

I'm thrilled when he unties the cups of my bra. My nipples are hard, and they pretty much salute anyone who walks by me. Right outside the men's locker room door, he says, "I'm going in the restroom. Stay right here," and clips my leash to a ring on the wall. As soon as he disappears, who should turn up but Steffen. Imagine that – what a coincidence. I shiver because I'm pretty sure this won't go well for me.

"Hey, little one! How are things going over at Master Clint's?"

I shake my head. "Sir, you're not supposed to be talking to me. You know that. Please don't get me in trouble. Please?"

"Don't you wish you'd come with me? That they'd drawn our names together? I do; I still do."

"Sir, please . . ."

"What the hell is going on here?" Clint walks out of the restroom and Steffen just smiles. I shrink and don't say anything.

"I was just telling your sub here that I wish they'd called our names together. I don't think you deserve her." Steffen leers at Clint, and I can see Clint's hackles rise.

"Is that right? That is now no longer an option, so just accept it, Steffen. By the way, where's the sub you drew?"

"Over at the bar. We're going to scene in a few minutes, so she's getting some liquid courage in her."

"You know you're not supposed to be talking to another Dom's sub. Thanks for following protocol." I can tell Clint is furious.

"Yeah, well, take it out on her. See you later, little one," Steffen says with a grin and turns to go to the bar.

"Sir, I didn't . . ."

"You know you're not supposed to talk to another Dom without my permission." He's glaring at me.

"I wasn't, Sir! I was trying to make him go away." I can feel myself start to tremble.

"You were flirting with him. Admit it."

That really pisses me off. "No, Sir, I wasn't! I was trying to get him to leave me alone. I said, 'Sir, you're not supposed to be talking to me,' but he just kept on."

"Come with me." He takes my leash and pulls me down the hallway to one of the private rooms. "You're going to learn protocol. You'll not be caught talking to another Dom again without my permission. I won't have it."

When we get into the room, I realize there's a huge frame sitting right in the middle of the space. There are eye bolts all around it and chains dangling from them. "Get in the frame. Hands above your head." He puts a pair of cuffs on my wrists. Then he pushes a block of wood up. "Stand on this." He clips the cuffs to the chains in the top of the frame and, before I can blink, he kicks the block out from under me.

I'm hanging by my wrists, my toes barely touching the floor. The sound of a drawer opening hits my ears, and then he moves behind me. He unhooks my top so my back is exposed, then pulls my shorts and thong down and off. "You'll learn to refrain from talking to other Doms. Count 'em."

I hear a whir and the pop of leather against my skin as some kind of whip strikes my back, and I shriek. It makes contact again, and his voice knifes into me. "I. Said. Count."

"Two, Sir!" The snap sounds off again, followed by the pain, and I shriek again.

"Three, Sir!" "Four, Sir!" "Five, Sir!"

By twenty I'm exhausted, both from dangling and from the pain. He keeps going and I realize I'm not shrieking now, just counting. At forty, I'm barely counting anymore – I can't make my voice work. By fifty, I'm trying to make sense of everything when I realize he's undoing my chains. Next thing I know, I'm on the bed with him and he's stroking my back tenderly with his fingers.

"Will you speak to another Dom without my permission again?"

"No, Sir. I will not," I whisper.

I feel him rubbing something on my skin, and he says, "Good. I expect you've learned that lesson on protocol." With that, he wraps his arms around me. "You took that very well. It's difficult to take a lashing with the flogger the first time, but you did it."

"Yes, Sir," is all I can whisper out.

In about ten minutes things are starting to make sense again. He helps me stand up and then pulls my top the rest of the way off. "No top. I want everyone to see your stripes and know you performed well. They're a badge of honor, Vännan."

I stand there for a few seconds, then say, "Sir, could I have permission to speak, please?"

He looks a little surprised. "Yes, Vännan. What is it?"

I look down at the floor. "Sir, for the record, I was *not* flirting with Master Steffen. He was trying to get me to say that I wanted to be paired with him. And he couldn't. I wouldn't say it because it would be a lie."

There's an unreadable look that passes over his face before he says, "Well, that's good to know." That's all he says. He takes my leash and leads me through the big room and back to the car.

Chapter 6

"Elbows and knees. I want to take your ass. I'm hoping for all night. Do you want it, Vännan?" I climb up into the bed eagerly.

"Yes, Sir! I want it very much, Sir."

"Good. You're going to get it. Over and over. And don't forget to let me hear your pleasure. If I don't, I'll assume you don't want it. No telling what I'll do then!" he chuckles and slaps my ass.

After he's come in me about eight times and left me hanging, he pulls out and lies down beside me. I'm still in the fucking position and he looks over into my face. "Come here, Vännan." I drop and roll into his side and, when I do, he rolls to face me and begins to stroke my clit. I moan and close my eyes until he says, "Eyes open! Look right into mine. I want to watch your face when you come."

I feel it coiling and growing bigger and bigger, and then it's on me, my body trembling and my hips churning, bumping against his hand as he continues to stroke my swollen bud. "Eyes open!" he barks again, and I stare straight into his, their heat making me blush as the climax overwhelms me. When he finally stops I'm a panting, sweating mess. And he surprises me by kissing my forehead. "I'm going to teach you something. Would you like that?"

"Yes, Sir! I would, very much."

"Spread 'em." I spread my legs wide. He stares down at me and shoves two fingers into my pussy. "This will be uncomfortable until you learn what's happening and how to let it go. Ready?"

"It would help if I knew what I'm supposed to be ready for, Sir."

"Have you ever squirted?"

Some of us subs at the club have whispered about it between ourselves. My eyes go wide. "No, Sir! Is it real? I've heard about it, but . . ."

"Well, you're about to. Try to relax." I take a deep breath and blow it out. He starts to stroke into me with the two fingers, and I feel something, an unusual something, like I've never felt before.

"Sir, what is . . ."

"That's your G-spot, sub. I'm ramping it up. It's going to feel like you need to pee, but you'll have to learn to let go." He starts finger fucking me like crazy.

A weird sensation takes me over. It's like I can't be still, my hips wiggling and bucking. I'm panting and writhing. "Let it go, little one. Come on. You can do it."

"But I don't want to pee . . ."

"It's not pee, precious. Let it go."

I concentrate. It seems unnatural to just let loose of my bladder, but I don't know what I'm supposed to do.

It's becoming unbearable, and he says, "Your gland is full. You've got to let go." He increases the speed of the strokes, and I start to cry out. "Let it go, Vännan."

I do; it makes me hideously uncomfortable to do so, but I still do. I hear him yell, "Yeah! That's it! You did it! Take a look."

The bed is soaked. My face is hot with embarrassment when he says, "Open your mouth." I do, and he stuffs both fingers into it. "Suck."

It's not urine. It's kind of sweet and musky. "What is that?" I ask when he pulls them out.

"It's female ejaculate. You just ejaculated. How did it feel?" He's put the heel of one hand on my mons and he's pressing – hard. All the sexual tension I felt in my pussy is disappearing.

"It was, I don't know, weird but intensely erotic. I want to do it again."

"Not tonight, babe. I've got to clean this up. Now go and clean yourself up a little, take a leak, and get back here. You're spending tonight in my bed." When I come back, he pulls a chain from the side of the bed and puts a cuff on me – one with a padlock. "Get some sleep," his lips murmur into the back of my neck, tickling me as he spoons against my back. "We've got quite a day ahead of us tomorrow.

"Come on. It's not that bad." I'm stumbling and tripping over roots and branches and all kinds of crap. I'm not much of an outdoor girl, and this is freaking me out a little.

We've been hiking for about an hour when I hear him say, "Aw, yeah! This is the place!" When I come out of the tree line, I gasp.

We're on a bluff above a huge lake. I might've hated the hike, but the view is breathtaking. The water is blue and the sky is too, filled with fluffy little clouds. Everywhere there's green, the trees, the grass, the edges of the water where the algae and stuff grows. It's gorgeous, and we're up in the air about eighty feet. "So what are we doing here, Sir?" I ask, unable to understand why we'd hike all the way out here just to look at a lake.

What the hell is wrong with me? I must be a special kind of stupid. I realize that when he tells me what to do.

"Take off everything. Then go and stand against that tree and look at me." He points to a tree that looks kind of, I don't know, rough? Scratchy? I undress and stand with my back against it. It's even scratchier than it appears, and its surface digs into my skin in an oddly exciting kind of way.

Once I undress and turn toward him, I'm rewarded with my own version of the greatest show on earth. He unbuckles his belt, then unbuttons his jeans and unzips them. Once they're undone, he pulls them down about twelve inches, then reaches up for the waistband of his boxer briefs. He pulls them down to meet the jeans, and his cock is free and pointing straight at me. It's glorious out there in the sun, a shiny little drop crowning its tip, and I want to lick it so badly that I can hardly stand it.

He walks toward me, his hand wrapped around his shaft as he pumps it in a slow stroking rhythm, tormenting me.

"Sir, I . . ."

"Want it, Vännan? It's waiting for you. Will you suck it here? In the wide open? It wants your mouth on it, little one."

"Yes, Sir. I want to suck it, Sir. Please?" I can't believe I'm begging, but it's so beautiful that I think I'll die if it's not *somewhere* in my body pretty soon.

"Come over here and kneel. Take it in." I practically run to him and drop to my knees in front of the cock I've grown to enjoy worshipping. I run my tongue up and down its length, then suck his balls before using my tongue again, and the rocks and sticks and leaves under my knees only add to the wildness I feel taking hold of me. He groans and wraps his fingers in my hair, and I know he's getting ready to slam down into my throat. But this time I'm wrong.

"Love my cock, Vännan. Love it with your lips, with your tongue. Make love to my cock, sweet baby. I want to feel you enjoying it." When my mouth goes down over its length he groans, and the sound pushes me across the line and into bliss.

I suck and lick, take it down deep, then suck and lick again, over and over. He's standing very still, and I wrap my arms around his thighs, then run them up and onto his ass, and he moans out, "God, those beautiful lips. They're swollen and blood red. Oh, baby, love my dick. It loves your mouth." His head is thrown back, eyes closed and face raised to the sun, and he's gorgeous, every inch of him. I take it very slow. I want it to last, for him to enjoy it as long as possible, and he seems to want the same thing.

I work on it for a long, long time, and watch as I suck it over and over and it gets bigger and harder and darker. I can feel the blood vessels in its length pulsing on my tongue. He's still standing rigid as a statue, letting me take him in and out of my lips, my teeth raking the head occasionally, and then he says, "Vännan, I want to come so I can fuck you. I know you want it too. Make me come, baby. Make me cry out."

I double my efforts, then start to actually stroke my throat down onto his shaft, the velvet head of his dick striking the soft back of my palate and wringing juices from my cunt with every slam. I go faster and deeper, then add a twisting motion at the base of his shaft with my hand, and he groans deep in his throat. With that, I feel it get more rigid and thick and my mouth is full of his seed, hot and bitter and creamy. I drink it all down as he cries out, "Oh, fuck! Oh my god, oh my god, ahhhhhhh." Hands in my hair, he holds my face down on his length, the bulbous head stuck down my throat, and I can't breathe but I don't care. I need him in me, anywhere I can get him.

When he pulls me off he points, "Over there on that rock. On your back. I want to fuck you for the whole world to see." Once I'm in place, he kneels beside the huge slab and buries his face in my slit, his tongue raking here and there, making me squeal and writhe.

Once he's pretty sure I'm crazed, he sinks his swollen shaft into me and I scream out, "Oh, god, Sir, fuck me! I need your cock, Sir!" He proceeds to do just that, ramming me over and over as we couple there, enjoying each other in the sunlight and breeze.

I hear a sound and look up to see a group of hikers, three men, watching us from the trail. I try to tell Master, but he's engrossed. Then he surprises me – apparently he'd already noticed them. "If you want to gawk," he pants out, "get on out here and watch me fuck her."

To my surprise, two of them turn away, but one walks right out and watches Clint fuck me there in the open air. Once he's become bold, the other two follow suit. I look up at Clint, mortified, but he looks down into my eyes and says, "Vännan, the only man here who's any of your concern is me. If you're pleasing me, that's all that matters."

"Are you pleased, Sir?" I smile up at him.

He smiles back down at me. Finally! "Yes, Vännan. I'm very, very pleased. Your pussy feels so incredible, and I love the fact that we're being watched." The only thing going through my mind is *I made him smile!* That's my biggest accomplishment of the day.

The guys continue to watch until we both come, and then he finger fucks me until I squirt. They seem to enjoy that, then they head back onto the trail. One of them is polite enough to call back, "Thanks for the show!" Clint starts to laugh, and then I do too.

"I have to ask, Sir, did you set that up too?" I'm pretty sure he did.

To my surprise, he says, "No. I've been here hundreds of times and I've never seen another soul here. Wouldn't you know?" He pulls me up off the rock, sits down on it, and holds me in his lap. "Did you enjoy this, Vännan?"

"Very much, Sir. I'm not much of an outdoors girl, but this was, well, over-the-top sexy. I love the feel of the sun and breeze on my bare skin."

"I love the look of the sun on your bare skin! And I enjoyed knowing that someone else watched me satisfy you. Ready to go back?"

Even though I don't really want it to end, I say, "I guess so." I lay my head over on his shoulder and he surprises me by kissing my cheek.

"Come on. I saw a place that has ice cream on our way. Want some?" he asks, setting me down and standing beside me.

"Only if I can rub it on your cock and lick it off, Sir," I grin.

He grins back. "I'm sure we can work something out!"

Not only do I rub it on his cock and lick it off, he drips it onto my cunt and does some licking of his own. We do it in the car like a couple of horny teenagers, and we giggle and laugh the whole time. When we're done we're a sticky mess, but we've had fun.

When we get back to the house, I put my hand on his where it rests on the steering wheel before he can get out. "Sir, I just want you to know that I had a lot of fun today. Thanks for showing me a good time."

He leans over and kisses my forehead. "You know, I had fun too, the most fun I've had in a long, long time." Then he comes around to open my car door and we go in the house, where I'm pretty sure he'll fuck me all night long.

At least I'm hoping so.

The bliss is short-lived. On Saturday afternoon apparently I commit another faux pas. When he comes into the living room to watch the ballgame, I'm kneeling on the floor in my spot. The first words out of his mouth are, "What the hell do you think you're doing?"

My eyes go round. "What, Sir? I don't know . . ."

"Your hair. Why did you do that?"

I just pulled it up into a ponytail after I washed it. I thought it would be nice, since it didn't appear we were going anywhere, and it would keep it out of the way. "Uh, Sir, I . . ."

"I thought you understood that it belongs to me. I don't want it tied up. I like it down. Go back there, take it down, brush it out, and get back out here. Pronto." I take off at a run, or as much of one as I can manage in heels, and do as he says. Then I come back out and drop back into my spot. I thought that settled it.

It did not.

He disappears and comes back with a pair of nipple clamps in his hand. "Stand in front of me and arch your back. Put your arms behind you and grab each elbow with the opposite hand." When I do, my boobs stick out and my nipples are front and center. He twists and sucks one until it's hard, then puts the clamp on it, and repeats with the other. Once they're on, he starts to turn a little screw device on them and they get tighter and tighter until tears are running down my cheeks. Then he grabs the chain and pulls me across the room.

When we get to the front door, I wonder if he's going to lead me out onto the porch naked, but he doesn't. Instead, he twists a loop into the chain and pulls it down, looping it over the doorknob. "You'll stay there until I tell you that you can move. And keep your arms behind your back."

It takes about fifteen seconds for the position to get uncomfortable, and less than two minutes for it to become unbearable. It wouldn't be so bad if I could use my hands to brace myself, but I can't; they're still behind me. It's becoming hard to stay upright on the heels when I'm bent over so far, but I know if I fall the clamps will probably rip my nipples right off.

He watches the first inning. Then the second inning. I can't believe I'd still be standing by the end of the third inning, but I am. Halfway through the fourth I'm beginning to think I won't be able to stand it another minute when he says, "Unloop the chain from the door and come over here." I do as he says and totter to him, still somewhat bent over and tears streaming down my face.

"Here we go," he says and pulls off the first clamp. The agony makes me lightheaded. I'm panting and screaming when he pulls off the second one, and I stumble and almost fall from the pain, but he catches me. "*Now* you can kneel." That's all he says, and he goes back to watching the game as though nothing has happened.

I look down at my nipples. They're purple and swollen, and they have little ridges in them where the clamps were. I desperately want him to suck on them, lick them, make them feel better, but he just keeps watching TV. At the end of the fifth inning he asks, "Still hurting?"

"Yes, Sir," I whine.

"You can reach them with your mouth, can't you?" he asks.

I nod. "Yes, they're big enough that I can, Sir."

"Suck and lick them yourself. And do it so erotically that I can't watch TV for watching you."

I start. At first I'm just flicking at them with my tongue, but then I start to actually suck them. They sag just enough that I can bring them up and capture them between my lips – hey, gravity is not my friend, okay? At first, he's paying absolutely no attention to me. As I suck one, I lick it, and I moan a little.

That gets his attention, and he unzips his jeans, pulls his briefs down under his balls, and starts to stroke his cock. I want to suck it so bad that I can't stand it, but he hasn't told me that I can, so I keep it up with my nipples. After a little while I draw them down, then roll and pinch them with my thumb and fingers. I pull on them individually a couple of times, then at the same time, then go back to sucking them, and I watch him start to stroke faster. A little groan escapes his lips and he rubs his palm around the suede-soft head of his dick, then goes back to stroking. I'm getting hot and wet watching him, and he's getting hot and hard watching me, and we're driving ourselves crazy watching each other. I take a chance.

"Sir, I'd love to suck your cock."

"I'm sure you would, but I want you to watch me pleasure myself instead. Does it arouse you to see me do this?"

"Yes, Sir. It's very, very hot." I pause, then I say, "You're very, very hot, Sir."

"Thank you, Vännan. You're pretty damn hot yourself. Bring those tits over here, baby." I crawl in between his legs and lean in, and he squeezes my breasts together and slips his cock between them. In a matter of seconds he's tit-fucking me like crazy and I'm still playing with my nipples. Watching me makes him frantic and he's thrusting like crazy. He cries out, "Oh, god, Trish, oh, fuck!" and shoots cum up under my chin, where it runs down all over my chest. When he stops panting, he looks down at my chest and smiles, then runs his finger through his cream and sticks it in my mouth. I give his finger a hard suck and he repeats the action, watching me with sparkling eyes while I suck his finger over and over until I've taken in almost all of his cum. "You'd lick it off your chest if you could reach it, wouldn't you, Vännan?"

"Yes, Sir, I would," I say, blushing a little and looking away.

In a flash his hands are on my waist, pushing me down onto the carpet, and he's in me and pumping like a maniac before I can even brace myself. My legs come up and around his waist, and he squeezes the flesh of my ass in his hands as he drives into me, his palms searing my skin, the ballgame forgotten in his frenzy to take me. "Reach between us and stroke yourself, baby. Make yourself come." I don't need to be told twice, and I start stroking my hard little nub and crying out, grinding against him with every thrust of his hips.

I finally scream out as I convulse, my cunt banging into his pelvis as he continues to slam into me, and he cries out, "Oh, fuck me!" I can't believe there could still be a drop of cum in him, but it shoots into me and runs back out as he continues to milk himself into me.

When he drops on top of me, his lips find my ear. "You are without a doubt the most precious, delectable fuck I've ever had," he whispers, nibbling at my earlobe, and I giggle. "Do I do it for you, little one? How do you feel when I fuck you, baby?"

"Like I can't get enough. Like you fill me up in ways no one else ever has. Like I don't want it to end, Sir." I want to say, *Like I'm falling for you,* but I don't.

"Then we're on the same page," he whispers back to me, and I feel something in my chest, something that makes me feel like a fifteen-year-old girl.

And I like it.

Chapter 7

Thursday passes without me getting myself into any of that trouble, you know, the kind that I seem to not know I'm getting into until I'm already there. Clint winds up having to do some work and, bless his heart, he falls asleep with his laptop in his lap, leaning over on the sofa. I wake him so he can go to bed; I just quietly say, "Sir. Sir, please, wake up and go to your bed. You're going to hurt in the morning if you don't." He takes me by the hand and leads me down the hallway to his room. We have sex, a calm, peaceful thing, then he promptly falls asleep. I'm not sure if he wants me there or not, but I'm afraid to get up and leave, so I just stay there with him. The next morning he wakes hard as flint, his head resting on my chest and my arms tight around him, and he seems glad to find that I'm still there. So it goes pretty well, all things considered.

Friday I'm not so lucky.

I keep thinking about the date. It seems like there's something I've got to do or somewhere I've got to go, but I can't remember what, and my planner is at home. Around ten that morning, after Clint's gone to meet with a client, I suddenly remember: I've got a doctor's appointment. Not just any doctor's appointment, but an appointment with a gynecologist it's taken me four months to get in to see. I've *got* to be there. And I have no car.

I try to call Clint, but he doesn't answer his phone. I'm frantic. By eleven, I don't know what to do so, since I'm ready to go, I call a cab. I make it there with ten minutes to spare and check in.

The appointment was at eleven forty-five. At one o'clock, I'm still waiting. Two o'clock comes and goes, and still nothing. I'm not the only one sitting around either. There's a whole waiting room full of patients, all sitting there for hours.

Sometime shortly after three, I get a text from Ron.

hey y is there a charge on my cc 4 over 2c at fet wear-house? wtf?

Clothes for my adventure, dickwad.

y should i pay for that?

Maybe because I worked to put you through college, asshat.

im calling my attorney skanky bitch

Community property state, ball licker. Suck on that. Now leave me tf alone. That should take care of his questions.

By four o'clock, I'm beginning to think this appointment isn't going to happen. At four fifty, they finally call my name. I see the sign on the door that reads "All cell phones turned off past this point," so I turn mine off. In the exam room I take off my clothes, put on the paper dress, and wait.

At six ten the doctor finally comes in. She apologizes profusely; she had a baby to deliver and there were complications. By now I'm no longer upset that I've had to wait so long. Instead, I'm upset that Clint will be home and I won't be there, and I don't know what will happen when I do get there.

I finally get out of there at six forty-three. I have two missed calls from Clint, and I try to call him, but he doesn't answer. I made the woman at the window in the doctor's office sign the receipt saying I was there until six forty so I have proof of where I was. The lights are on when I get to the house, and I gingerly step through the doorway, wondering what manner of hell is about to descend on me.

Clint is in the kitchen, making something that smells delicious. When I come in, I'm about to cry. He turns and asks, "So where have you been?" He doesn't seem angry, and I'm relieved.

"I kept thinking that I had somewhere I was supposed to be, Sir, and then I remembered about ten o'clock that it was a doctor's appointment, and it was with a doctor I've been trying to get in to see for four months."

"And what time was this appointment?" he asks.

"Eleven forty-five. And I just left there. See? The woman at the window signed it so you'd know I was there." I show him the receipt.

His brow furrows in disgust. "Did the physician give you any idea why you had to wait so long?"

"Yes. She said she had a baby to deliver but the delivery was complicated and it took longer than she thought. I wasn't the only one waiting. There was a whole waiting room full of women waiting to see her."

"I see." That's all he says. He turns back to the stove.

"So is it okay, Sir? I mean, are you angry, Sir?" I've finally stopped shaking.

"Sure. It's okay. I mean, you couldn't help it, right?" He stirs something and then gets out a plate.

"No, Sir, I couldn't, but I'm sorry I didn't remember sooner. I did try to call you, Sir, several times, but you didn't answer and I didn't know what to do, so I got a cab." I realize I'm starting to babble, but I'm just trying to explain.

"Um-hum," he says kind of absent-mindedly. I can't believe it's okay. I thought he'd have my head.

"So everything is all right, Sir?" I'm still shaking a little.

"Of course." He begins to put food on a plate. Notice I said plate, the singular form. There's only one plate.

It registers, but I try to make light of it and smile. "So what's for dinner, Sir?"

"Oh, let's see, sautéed chicken breast, roasted broccoli, and yellow squash."

"Sounds good, Sir. I'll get a plate too."

That's when the other shoe falls. "Oh, I didn't make enough for you."

I stare at him. "Wha . . . What do you mean?"

He doesn't crack a smile, doesn't even look at me. "I didn't know when you'd be back so I didn't cook you anything."

"Sir, I didn't know when I'd be back either or I would've left you a message. And they required me to turn off my phone when I was there, so I couldn't call you."

He turns to look at me and, face passive and cold, he says, "You could've at least left a note telling me where you'd gone. I had no idea where you were. So I only cooked for myself." He turns to go to the table, leaving me standing there.

"That's okay, Sir. I'll just fix myself something," I say, opening the refrigerator.

"Nope. Kitchen's officially closed."

I feel like a seven-year-old. He's going to make me go without supper.

"You're kidding, right?" I can't believe it. "Even if I cook it? Why isn't that okay?"

He turns and looks at me, and there's no mirth in those eyes, just coldness, his voice forcing an icy chill into my core. "You will watch your bratty, impertinent tone with me, sub. You know your place. Get to it." With that, he turns and starts eating.

After I go into my bedroom and take everything off, I put on my heels and collar and go to kneel in the living room. He finishes eating and spends the rest of the evening ignoring me. At bedtime, he doesn't even speak.

I find myself wishing he'd yell at me instead of just ignoring me. He gets ready for bed, so I just sit there, feeling like The Invisible Woman. Finally, at about midnight, he appears in the living room. And all he says is, "Go to bed." Then he turns and leaves the room.

Once he's in his room with the door closed, I get up and go down the hall to my room. I brush my teeth and hair, wash my face, and climb into bed. Even though it's summertime, it's cold in that bed. He hasn't touched me since he left for his meeting this morning. I don't know if he'll want me to come in and pleasure him in the morning, so I go ahead and set my clock. I try to go to sleep, but I toss and turn and generally ache all over.

I must've eventually dozed off, because at six the alarm clock goes off. Getting up and tiptoeing down the hall to his room, I find the door closed. Thinking I'd better be polite, I give a timid knock. There's no answer. I knock a little louder; still no answer. I finally get worried. What if something's wrong, or he's overslept? So I crack the door open and peek in.

He's not there. The bed is empty. It's been made. The kitchen is cleaned up, the dishes in the dishwasher. I check the coffee pot; it's still a little warm, so he had coffee. But he didn't wake me to suck him or to even eat a little breakfast with him.

I spend the day trying to catch up some laundry I'd intended to do the day before, then empty trash cans and mop the kitchen floor. The whole day is shrouded in uncertainty. Mid-afternoon I read a little, then take a nap. I wake at four and decide I'd better look around to see what I can find to make for dinner. I haven't eaten all day; I haven't had an appetite.

There are plenty of beans and crushed tomatoes in the pantry, and in the freezer I find meat, so I can make chili, no problem. After it's together and started, I look at the clock. It's five thirty and I haven't heard from him. At six I start to get worried, so I call him – no answer. By seven the chili's about to burn, so I turn it off. Eight comes around and then nine, and nothing. I don't know what to do. At ten, still not having heard from him, I go in and kneel in my spot.

When I realize it's midnight and he's still not there, I do something very uncharacteristic for me. I start to cry. I'm pretty sure he's not coming home, and I wonder where he is and what he's doing. What if something's happened to him?

My phone starts ringing a little after midnight and I run to it, but it's Sheila, so I don't even answer it. I finally lean forward and stretch out, my torso almost resting on the floor, arms straight out, and cry into the carpet. I've started to get scared and I don't know what to do.

Time just disappears, and my mind is in a haze. Things had been going so well, and then I do something so stupid that I can't even believe I did it. I'm still stretched out there, sobbing, when I hear the door. I don't even look up; I don't think I can.

I hear him drop his keys in the bowl by the door and set his messenger bag down. He doesn't speak to me, doesn't touch me, nothing, just walks by me and goes down the hall, closing the bedroom door behind him. I'm so confused that I just stay there. I don't know how to apologize more than I already have, and I can't undo what I did. But at least I know he's safe. That's all I really care about.

I wake to the sound of him moving around in the kitchen and sunlight pouring into the front window. When I try to move, I find my joints so stiff that I can't. I'm in the same position I've been in for over six hours and I'm aching. After some work, I finally make it up to kneeling position. I haven't had anything to eat since two mornings previous, and nothing to drink since about seven the night before. I'm feeling kind of weak and very, very tired, not to mention the aching. In a few minutes Clint appears in the doorway with, thank god, two cups of coffee in his hands. I wonder if he's doing it just to torture me, but thankfully he brings both cups to the coffee table, sets them down, and in a voice soft and sweet says, "Vännan, come to me."

It's difficult to stand, so I just crawl on my knees, carpet burn be damned. When I get to the sofa I try to get up, but I can't. I start to cry, and strong hands lift me. Next thing I know I'm sitting in his lap. Before he can say anything I cry out, "I was so scared!" Then I start to weep.

His voice is calm and soothing. "Do you understand now how worried I was when I got home and you weren't here? And there was no note? And you didn't answer your phone?" I nod. "We're not talking about Dom/sub protocol here, Vännan. We're talking common courtesy, that's all."

That's when I start to sob. "I know, but I was in such a hurry that I didn't even think about it, and I couldn't have dreamed it would be that late before I got back. I thought I'd be back home before you even knew I was gone. I'm so, so sorry. I didn't mean to . . ."

"Shhh, shhh." He presses my face to his shoulder. "It's okay, it's okay. Don't cry." He pulls my head up so he can look into my face and wipes my eyes with his hand. "But you remember this lesson, how it felt to not know where I was or if I was okay, to not know if or when I'd be back. And then to be ignored all evening . . ." When I shudder with a sob, he whispers, "That was hard for me too. You're hard to ignore, little one. Do you know that?" That makes me completely break down, and he pulls me to him and rocks me forward and back like a child.

Finally he says, "Here. Sit up and drink this. It'll make everything better. And let's go into the kitchen and get something to eat, okay? I know you're hungry." After drinking about half of the cup, I stand from his lap and let him lead me into the kitchen. I'm so hungry and tired that I can barely sit up, and he fixes me a big bowl of oatmeal with strawberries in it, which I promptly devour. He's still eating his, so I sit there while he eats, saying nothing.

I put our bowls in the sink and run water in them – I just don't have the strength to wash them right at that minute. Then the clock catches my eye: Eight forty-five. "Oh god, sir! You're late and everything! I'm so sorry – it's all my fault! I'll help you, okay?" I start rushing around, picking things up, making sure his bag is by the door, running through the morning checklist in my mind, so crazed that I can't speak.

"Hey! Hey, baby, stop. Stop, okay?" I'm so frantic that he finally takes my upper arms and turns me toward him. "Trish, just stop. It's okay." I stare at him. "I'm not doing any work today. That's the beauty of being your own boss. I cancelled a couple of things so I can stay here with you today." I start to cry again. "Oh, baby, you're just exhausted. Go get a quick shower and come back to my bed." It's a challenge to make it down the hall to my bathroom, but I manage.

When I've finished my shower and brushed my teeth, I stumble back up the hall to his room. He's in the bed, naked, waiting for me. I assume he wants me to suck him like I'm supposed to in the morning, but instead he braces himself above me. "Wrap your legs around me, Vännan." Once I have, he rolls us both to our sides and begins to pump into me slowly as though he's contemplating every fraction of an inch of flesh between us, kissing me softly on my forehead, stroking my hair. A couple of times while he's stroking into me I almost fall asleep. When I fight it, he lays a palm on my cheek and whispers, "Go ahead, baby. Go to sleep. Let me relax you enough for you to fall asleep." I just let go and feel his cock moving inside me, almost hypnotically. My consciousness begins to drift in and out. I feel him press into me and groan, and his cum warms my sheath. And that's it – I'm gone.

When I wake I look at the clock: Two twenty-three in the afternoon. Clint's asleep beside me. He rouses when I look at the clock and says, "Babe, if you need to go to the bathroom, go ahead." I almost crawl in there, relieve myself, and crawl back. In just a few seconds I'm back in his arms, my head pressed against his chest.

By the time I wake again, it's almost five o'clock. Clint isn't in the bed. I find him in the living room, reading a magazine article.

"There's the sleepyhead. Are you hungry?"

"Yes, Sir. I'm very hungry, Sir," I say, still in a daze and stretching.

"Go and throw something on. Nothing fancy. No underwear or bra. We'll go out and get something to eat." I go down the hall to my room and find a little sundress. Once I've pulled it on with a pair of sandals, I go back to the living room. "Well, don't you look cute? Let's go," he says, smiling at me. When I get to the door, I stop and let him open it for me. He smiles again and then leads me down the steps, opening the car door for me when we get there and helping me in.

We go down the street to a pizza place. As we sit there we chat about benign things, the weather, whether or not the mail carrier left anything in the box, how blue the sky has been today, and I start to feel a little better. After we eat, we stroll out of the pizza place but he doesn't go to the car. Instead, he heads down the sidewalk and motions for me to come with him. When I catch up, he takes my hand, and I'm surprised at how good it feels to hold his.

There's a park two blocks down, and there's no one there when we get there. He sits on a park bench. I start to sit beside him, but he shakes his head. He unzips his fly, pulls out his dick, and says, "Mount me facing forward." I simply pull up the hem of my dress and back onto him, sitting on his lap with his cock buried in my already-soaked pussy.

"Move on me, sub," he whispers, and I start to stroke up and down on his length, making sure to keep my dress down. He reaches up, wraps his arms around me, and begins to toy with my nipples through my dress. I see people coming from a distance, but he doesn't stop. It's an older couple, and when they get close, Clint whispers, "Get still."

They walk by but, to my surprise, after they've passed us the old man turns around and grins at Clint. A gasp escapes my lips. "Oh my god, he knew what we were doing!"

"Yeah. He'd like to be doing it too. Start again, baby. Ride me." In a couple of minutes I'm lost in ecstasy, and he comes in me like a tidal wave. I'm worried that I'll leave a mess on the front of his jeans, but he doesn't seem to care.

On the way home he asks, without looking at me, "All good?"

I nod my head. "Yes, Sir. It's all good. And I really am sorry, Sir."

"It's over. Let's just move forward, okay? Tomorrow is another day."

Yes it is. Thank god.

Chapter 8

Saturday is our compulsory day. We're required to go to the club and have an interview to report on how things are going. Clint acts like he's nervous, but I'm not sure why, and I have to wonder if he's worried about what I might say.

We're supposed to be there at one thirty. There's a deli downtown that I've always loved, and when I mention it, Clint wants to take me there.

I can't figure him out. Sometimes it seems like he wants me here and can't wait to spend time with me, and other times he acts like I'm nothing, or that I'm the last person he'd want to see. The yanking back and forth is tiresome. I plan to say that to whoever is interviewing us.

When we get to the club there are a couple of other Dom/sub pairings there waiting for their interviews. They put each pair in a private room to wait, and we wind up in Dave's office because it's the only room left. He's got some little trinkets on his desk, and I play with a couple of them while we're waiting. When he comes to the doorway, he sighs and says, "Okay, you two, who's first?"

Clint points at me. "Ladies first!" he laughs, but underneath it he still seems nervous. Once I'm seated in the main commons room on one of the leather sofas, I look around.

"Looks a lot different with all the lights on!" I giggle, and Dave grins at me. "So, what do we do?"

"We just talk. How do you think it's going?"

"In what way?"

"Let's try again. How's the sex?" That's Dave, blunt as hell.

I nod. "The sex is good – very good. Great, in fact. We've done things I never thought I'd do." That was sure true.

Dave's face clouds. "No hitches? He hasn't used sex as punishment, has he?"

"Discipline maybe, but not punishment. He told me up front he doesn't believe in that."

"Good." He seems relieved. Does he know something I don't? "How about getting along? Do you seem to get along okay?"

I think for a minute. "I didn't think so at first, but he's been a lot warmer to me over the last couple of days. I'm a whole lot more comfortable around him." I stop, not knowing if I should say what I was about to. Then I decide to go for broke. "But there is something that bothers me a lot."

His brows shoot up. "Oh? What's that?"

I shake my head. "He's either hot or cold. There's no in between. He's either mad at me and doesn't even want to look at me, or he's all lovey-dovey and wants to cuddle and I'm his best friend. It's hard to handle, Dave. I never know what'll set him off."

He nods. "I understand. In his defense, he is responsible for teaching proper protocol and enforcing rules. But otherwise, that's something he and I need to address. Be aware that after he and I talk, you may get called back in for a discussion regarding something he's said." I nod. "But I understand what you're talking about. I like to know how I'm going to be received when I walk up to someone."

"Exactly." I can see Dave understands.

"Are you having any trouble with any of the house protocol? Feel like there's anything that's really not fair?"

"Not really. It's all pretty average stuff, pick up after yourself, rinse out your washcloth, stuff like that. No big deal. I'm still trying to get used to the 'nude' rule though." I think about Clint's kids. "How do people with kids do this?"

"It's difficult. They have to keep their D/s stuff under wraps, practice it when the kids are away or asleep. But it can be worked out." He thinks for a minute. "Has he shared anything of his history with you yet?"

"No. I know he has two girls, but that's all. He practically threatened me with death if I asked him about his marriage, and he let me know he wasn't interested in mine." Dave frowns at this. "I know his kids have a bedroom and I'm not supposed to open the door. I know his mother has them right now. And I know they're not coming back until I'm gone. So I don't know that any of it matters anyway."

"Yes, it matters. It matters a lot. I think he and I have a lot to talk about. So, Trish, here's the big question." Dave sits back in the chair and folds his arms across his chest. "If Clint were to ask to collar you, what would you say?"

I wondered if this would come up and, even though I've thought about it, I still don't have an answer. "Honestly, I don't know. I mean, I like him a lot. But I don't think he likes me. Well, maybe he likes me better than he did before, but still not much. I wouldn't think that's a question I even have to consider."

"I think you should." What? Really? Surely not. "If not Clint, who? Is there anyone you'd consider allowing to collar you?"

I shrug. "Maybe Steffen, but I don't know."

"Were you hoping your name would be drawn with Steffen's?"

I've asked myself that a million times. I shrug again. "At first I think I was glad it was Clint. But after some of the things that have happened and the indifferent way he's treated me at times, I started thinking about Steffen. He doesn't strike me as someone whose personality is a toss-up. He seems pretty even-tempered."

"But you said things have been better between you and Clint."

"They have. I pulled a stupid stunt the other day, well, not really, it didn't start out as one but it turned out that way. He punished me . . . and it was pretty harsh. Then afterward, he was very kind and sweet, and we've had a good time since then. He was very careful to make me see how I would've felt if he'd done the same thing I did; actually, he intentionally did something similar to drive home his point. And it's been fine since." I stop, then add, "But I feel like I'm always waiting for the other shoe to drop."

"Do you think he's helped you grow sexually? Really pushed your limits?"

"Yeah, I do. He set some things up that really threw me for a loop, but they were good learning experiences. He's very erotically creative. Sometimes he fucks me hard and uses me like a slut, even talks to me like one, and other times he's quiet and gentle and it feels like he's making love to me." I look down at my hands. "It's very confusing. I really don't know what's going on most of the time."

"But do you think this is a positive experience?" Dave sounds almost apologetic.

I think for a minute. "Yeah. I do. But for the wrong reasons."

"What do you mean?"

"I think it's really helping me see what I *don't* want in a Dom. And I'm really sad about that." Then something shoots through my brain and I panic. "Oh, god, please tell me you're not going to tell him what I say!" I'll be in trouble for sure.

Dave's face takes on a concerned look. "No plans to, just general discussion with him. But I think I'd like to call the two of you in together and talk to you. Can you do that?"

A tremor runs through my body and I'm pretty sure Dave sees it. "You have to make him promise not to punish me for the things I say or I just can't say anything."

Dave's shoulders square. "You just let me know if he even tries and I'll put a stop to it. That's against the code. I'll not have that. You don't have to be afraid, Trish. Clint's not that unfair."

Yeah? He should have to be Clint's sub for two weeks. He might sing a different tune.

When we're done, Dave hugs me and says, "Go back over to my office and send Clint over. And thanks, honey."

"No, thank you. I love you, Dave." I realize what I've said, and then I throw in, "You know, like you're, well, it's more . . ."

He laughs. "Don't worry, little one. I love you too. You're just special to me, and I know I'm special to you."

I hug him again. "You are. You always will be."

Once I've pointed Clint across the hallway, I settle in to wait. The pictures Dave has around on the walls are interesting, and I look at them for awhile. I peruse his bookshelf; not the books I thought I'd see. Instead of *The History of Bondage in America*, he has a couple of Stephen King books and some Dean Koontz. I tear a piece of paper off his notepad and doodle, but that's boring. But when I glance over at his credenza, I see something I hadn't noticed before.

The envelopes with the pairings in them.

I know every couple has a number, but I don't know what ours is. I rifle through, trying to find some kind of order, and then I figure it out: It's the order in which we're being interviewed. I know there are five couples after us, so that should make us sixth from the back. I pull the envelope, listening carefully for footsteps or voices, and open it.

There's my card. And with it . . .

Steffen Cothran. What the fuck? I don't understand. I pull open the next envelope and it's two names I don't recognize; same for the next. The third after me opens and there's Clint's card. The name with it is Katrina Brandon. She's the sub Steffen's got for the two weeks.

I hurry and put the envelopes back in the right order, then sit down and try to figure out what's going on. But I know one thing for sure.

Dave threw the drawing. He wanted us together, but I'm not sure why. Does Clint know? If he did, would he say anything? Was it his idea? I'm pretty sure the answer to that question is no. I'm still sitting there, reeling, when Clint opens the door. "He wants us together," he says without a hint of emotion.

I follow him up the hall and back into the big room. Clint waits until I sit before he does. Then Dave begins. "I really thought I should get the two of you together in here and talk. Trish, you brought up some things that were bothering you. I think you should tell Clint about them." I sit, mute. "Go on, honey. The two of you need to air this."

It's impossible for me to look at Clint, but I should keep my eyes averted anyway, so it's okay. I sit for awhile before I'm able to say, barely above a whisper, "Sometimes it seems like you really like me, and sometimes it seems like you want me anywhere but near you. And it's hard to spend time with someone when I don't know how they're going to treat me from one minute to the next."

He doesn't say anything for quite some while – at least two minutes. The wait is terrifying. When he does, he starts with, "Trish, look at me." When I finally look up at him – and it's hard to do so – he says, "Sometimes I don't know if I want you around or not."

Wow. Why don't you tell me how you really *feel?*, I want to scream, and I feel my lip begin to tremble. "If you don't want . . ." I start, but he stops me with a finger to my lips.

"Honey, I've got a lot of issues. I'm still having a very hard time. It's not you, it's me." He stops and his cheeks turn pink.

"Yeah, but it's not fair to take it out on me," I tell him.

"I didn't realize you thought that I was. I don't think I have, but I'll be more careful about that from now on. I don't want you to think I don't care about you, because I do. I want this to be a positive experience for you, and I want you to learn all you can." He pats my knee and leaves his hand there. I can feel its warmth through my jeans.

"Okay. I guess." I don't know what else to say. "But I never know if you're going to kiss me or kill me. It's hard to be around someone like that."

He nods. "I will admit I come across like that, I'm sure. Again, not you – me. But as your Dom, I should be the one constant in your life, the one point of contact you can always trust and confide in, the one person you're always sure has your best interests at heart. I'm guessing you haven't felt that way. I'm really sorry, and I need to work on that. Fair?" he asks. I nod. "I really do like you, Trish. I feel more comfortable with you than I have with anyone else. If nothing else, I'd like for this to end with us being friends and you feeling like you can call on me if you need anything."

"I'd like that too. I really do like you too, Clint." I want to say, *I think I'm falling in love with you*, but no way would I do that.

"That makes me feel good," he says as he smiles at me. I have to admit, I love to see him smile.

"Now, Trish, Clint has some things he needs to say to you. Go ahead," he says, motioning to Clint.

"You're far too concerned with what others think. I don't mean just about when we're scening publicly; I mean what others think about how you look or what you're saying. There's nothing wrong with you. You're a lovely person, and I want you to know that you don't have to worry about what anyone thinks. I do think you've gotten over some of the stage fright sexually, though. The incident with the hikers was an eye-opener for me. You've grown in your openness and you're really beginning to own your sexuality. You should be proud." He gives me a tiny little smile – god, he's sexy when he does that.

"Thanks. That's a nice thing to say," I manage and try to smile back.

"One thing that does bother me is your flirting. A Dom won't put up with that."

I frown. "I didn't realize I was flirting. I don't mean to." That's the truth.

"Maybe you're not, but it certainly seems that way to me. That incident with Steffen . . ."

"I *told* you, I wasn't flirting with him. He was flirting with me and I was trying to get him to go away. I didn't want to get in trouble." He starts to say something, but before he can, I say, "And before you tell me that I must have invited it in some way, let me assure you that I didn't even know he was anywhere around until he started in on me. It seemed like he just came out of nowhere. And regardless, if you'll remember, you punished me – fifty lashes. And made me walk through the club so everyone could see. Even though I didn't do anything wrong. So even though I wasn't flirting, I would never do it again if I were. Which I *was not*." I'm almost panting by the time I finish.

"I'd really like for it to stop." That's all he says.

"Okay. Well, let's try this. If you think I'm flirting, tell me. I want to know what I'm doing that looks like flirting to you so I can stop. Will you do that? Because I don't know what else to do."

"Yes. I'll gladly do that if you think it will help."

"Well, I'd much rather you told me so I can figure it out than to keep accusing me of it when I'm not doing it, at least not to my knowledge." I'm feeling a little shaky now.

Clint reaches over and takes one of my hands. "It's okay. We can work on it. Don't get upset with me, please?" I nod.

"Anything else?" Dave asks.

Clint looks a little embarrassed. He looks directly into my eyes and says, "If we're making lo . . . having sex, and I use your real name, I'd like it if you'd do the same for me."

I'm wondering where that came from. "Okay, that's doable. I just didn't want to be labeled impertinent."

He chuckles. "Won't happen, I promise. But I'd really like that, okay?"

"Sure! Not a problem." For some reason, that makes me very, very happy.

"So!" Dave says, slapping his knees. "Master Clint, do you have a lot more adventurous things planned for our girl here?"

"I do indeed. But she'll have to wait to see what they are," he says and winks at me. He's never winked at me before. I take that as a good sign. "Looking forward to that, Vännan?"

"Yes, Master, I am."

"Good!" Dave seems satisfied. "You two go on. I think if there are any other issues you'll work them out. You've got another week. Make the most of it." With that, he escorts us out of his office and goes in search of the next couple.

We walk to the car in silence, but once we're both in, Clint turns to me. There's a serious look on his face, one unlike the other serious looks he wears, and he asks with hesitation, "Trish, can you tell me exactly why you came into the lifestyle? Why is it that you're looking for a Dom?"

I think for a minute, and then I try to articulate it, but it's hard. "Well, I sort of fell into it. Literally. I kinda fell onto Dave in a bar and he gave me a card for the club. But when I got here, it seemed like, I don't know, like I'd been looking for something and it felt like I'd found it. Do you know what I mean?"

He nods. "But what do you want in the long run? What can the lifestyle give you that a plain vanilla relationship can't?"

There's no good way to describe it, but I know the answer. "I'm not looking for someone to just love or have a relationship with. I'm looking for someone to *bond* with, seriously bond with. I'm looking for someone who can fill a spot in my life that no one else can, someone I can trust. And I want it to be with someone who'll stretch me, help me reach my fullest potential, won't let me stagnate. Someone who'll offer me enough that I wake up every morning happy to see what the day will bring, not dreading the same old ho-hum thing. I'd like a little adventure, that's all." I stop and look at his face; he's watching me intently, his eyes never leaving mine. "Does that make sense?"

He starts the car and puts it in gear, his face never giving away his feelings. "Makes perfect sense. All the sense in the world," he says and pulls out onto the street.

"It works like this." He fills the soft plastic bottle and hands it to me. I hold it and squirt it out the little holes. "Three times. There are three in the package. Empty the stuff that's in them, rinse them thoroughly, and fill them with warm water. Think you can do that?"

Clint's teaching me proper techniques in anal sex preparation. I had no idea this was part of it all and I'm a little surprised Dave didn't teach me this earlier, so I blurt out, "I didn't know I was supposed to do this, Sir. I'm sorry for before now." This is embarrassing, and I feel my face burning.

"No one taught you. I've just dealt with it up until now. But you need to know how to do this." He leans up against the vanity in my bathroom. "Go ahead, try it."

"Here? With you standing there?" Now my face *is* burning.

"Yes. With me standing here. I fuck it, for god's sake. What difference does it make?" He's got a look on his face that tells me he can't understand my trepidation. I put the bottle and wand under me and try to line up the wand with my asshole. Once it starts in, I must make a face because Clint says, "As far in as you can make it go, which should be all the way. Then just squeeze but try to keep your hand out of the way."

It's grossly uncomfortable, but when the water runs out, so does some stuff I really didn't want to see. "Please, god, tell me that's not been . . ."

"A little bit. It's to be expected. But not anymore. The next bottle, please." I do the same thing again, and less comes out with the water this time. "One more time." The third bottle goes into me, and this time it comes out clear. "Perfect! Now it's my responsibility. If I want you to do this, I have to tell you beforehand. Do *not* do this unless I tell you to. It's not good for your body to do it every night, so if I want to fuck your ass, I'll tell you and you can prepare. If I don't tell you and decide I want to take you anally, that's my issue, not yours. Understand?"

"Yes, Master." *That wasn't so bad*, I think. *I don't mind it at all.*

"Good. Now I want to fuck that squeaky-clean ass of yours," he grins. Before I can get up, he holds me down on the toilet seat and squats down in front of me, his eyes level with mine. "Trish, I know some of this doesn't seem very sexy, but trust me, I find it very sexy that you'd prepare yourself for me this way. It shows me that you take my comfort and satisfaction seriously. And I appreciate it."

I'm shocked that he's said any of that. "Um, thanks. No, wait, you're welcome." He chuckles. "I don't really know how to respond to that."

"Just say, 'Master, I want you to fuck my ass,'" he laughs.

I start to laugh. "Master, I want you to fuck my ass," I repeat. "Right now!"

There's lots of squealing when he grabs me up, throws me over his shoulder, and plunks me down on the bed. "Kneel up close to the headboard and use it to hold yourself upright. Now arch your back to give me access to your pretty little pucker." I do exactly as he says, and he coats his cock with lube and shoves it into me. I moan out and clutch the headboard.

He fucks up into my rear entrance while his hands wind around my torso, his fingers gripping my nipples. He squeezes and twists them mercilessly, and I'm overcome with fire and heat, moaning and crying out, wanting every inch of him deeper and harder. If it were dark in the room, I truly believe the sparks from his hands on my skin would be visible. The pounding he gives me is insane, and I beg him for release. In response, he continues tormenting one nipple while he reaches down to my clit and strokes it with the other hand. "Keep your back arched!" he barks as he strokes my plump nubbin, and I writhe and grind against him as his dick plunges hard and deep into me.

"Master, may I come?" I pant out.

"No! You'll wait for me." I do, and I'm glad. In just a couple of minutes he grunts out, "Come for me, sub!" and I explode just as he unloads into my tight little hole, his white-hot batter filling me to overflowing. After he's thrust into me several more times, he says, "Lie down. I'll be back in a minute." I hear him in the bathroom taking a piss, and then the water running, and I know he's probably washing his cock. He doesn't want to take any chances of spreading bacteria into my vagina, and I appreciate that.

When he comes back, he says, "May I ask you a question?"

"Sure!" He wants to know something about me? That's a first.

"How old are you?"

Hell – I hadn't thought it would be that. "Um, forty-nine. How old are you?"

"Thirty-five." I almost gasp. He's younger than I thought. Guess it's that always-serious look on his face that makes him seem older. Then he asks the obvious question. "Trish, does that bother you? Being with a younger man?"

I shake my head. "No! Of course not. I'm flattered, really."

"You shouldn't be. You've got a beautiful body. You should be proud." He smiles at me and I blush. I've never thought of myself as being anything other than somewhat attractive.

"Does it bother you? Being with someone older, I mean?"

"Nope. None of anyone's business, and I like the way you look and feel. Your age isn't a problem for me.

I'm happy for that, but I'm puzzled. Why in the world would it matter? I've only got another six days and then he'll send me away. So who cares?

Chapter 9

"Okay, I'm getting ready to go in. Try to relax." Clint's cock is buried in my pussy, and I feel the dildo he's holding breach my rosette. As he shoves it in, he withdraws his shaft, then alternates over and over. Controlling my moaning isn't even possible anymore. "Doing okay?"

"Yeah, oh god, Master, it's so good!" I've never done anything like this. What's more, I find it unbelievably arousing that we're in bed and having sex at eleven o'clock in the morning. It feels like we're skipping school or work. "Oh god. Please don't stop doing that, okay?"

"Won't. I'm about to change it, though. Both will go in and out at the same time. It'll hurt the first few times, but it'll get better."

I start to say something when his dick and the dildo both stroke into me at the same time and I cry out, "Sweet mother of god, fuck me!" and shudder all over. My fingers are gripping the sheets furiously, and I feel like I'm going to split apart. "Oh god! Oh, it burns!" He slaps me on the ass with his free hand. "Oh god, Master, fuck me hard!" I can't stop myself from crying out. It's easily the greatest fucking I've ever gotten.

"I'm turning up the volume. Let me hear your pleasure, sub." He starts a more vigorous pumping and I'm lost in the deliciousness of the pain. I'm stretched to the max, so much so that I can barely breathe. He's working his cock and that dildo and I don't want it to ever stop. Then he reaches his free hand around me and starts to stroke my clit.

"Oh, god, Master, no! Please, oh no, please? Oh, god, fuck me, no, no, no. Yes! Oh, yeahhhhhh!" I'm squirming in my need, wanting more and afraid at the same time. The building of the orgasm is fast and furious.

Above my cries I hear, "Come for me, sub!" and my body turns loose. He's pounding his shaft and the dong into me hard and deep, and my cunt tries to clamp down but it can't – it's stretched too tight. I'm screaming out over and over, and he keeps going until I'm hoarse and shaking all over, then stops rubbing my clit, drops the dildo, and leans down onto my back. "I take my pleasure now, sub," he whispers to me as he wraps both arms around my waist and starts to hunch me like a wild animal mating. It's raw and primal and exhilarating. His balls slap my clit as he pounds into my warmth and wetness, then squeezes me even tighter and grunts his climax into me, banging my cervix as he does. He shoves in as far as he can go and shakes me with his efforts to drain his essence completely into me. Then he falls onto my back and lies there, arms around my waist.

My arms are shaking from weakness and from resting on them for so long, not to mention his body weight. Once he's beside me on the bed, he grabs me and yanks me down onto him, wrapping his arms around me. "How was that, Vännan? Was that good?"

"Oh, god, Master, that was incredible." I'm still burning, but it's a good burn.

"Wait until next time. Maybe next time you can be with me and . . . with two Doms," he corrects himself. My heart sinks. Two Doms, neither one of whom is him.

"Yeah, that would be great," I say, trying to fake excitement. This is my ninth day with him and he's still just as distant as he was the very first day. Warmer, yeah, but still distant. "Can I go to the bathroom, Master?"

"Sure! Go on," he says and slaps my ass as I get up. I go to the bathroom, pee, and throw some water on my face. When I go back to the bed, he's lying there, propped up on one elbow, and he smiles as he sees me come back.

"What?" I ask.

"Do you have any idea how beautiful and sexy you are? You're poetry in motion," he says, patting the bed beside him.

"Poetry in motion, Sir? Perhaps you haven't seen me walk in heels!" I laugh. It's true; I'm a lot of things, but graceful isn't one of them. I drop down on the bed beside him and prop myself to mirror his position, putting my face just inches from his.

"I have, and you're still poetry in motion. You've learned so much, Trish. I'm so impressed with you."

Impressed enough to collar me?, I wonder. Nope. I'm pretty sure that's the right answer to that question.

"Thank you, Master. You're a good teacher."

He acts like he's not sure what to say. Finally, he answers, "Thank you, Trish. I'm trying, really I am."

"I know, Master. It's not even noon. What are we doing for the rest of the day?"

"I need a new car. I wanted to go look at some. Want to go with me?" he asks, running a finger up and down my arm.

"Sure! That sounds like fun, Sir." Cars. I love cars. This will be great.

"Okay. I'll pick out your clothes. No panties, no bra. And stilettos." I groan. "But they make your legs look über sexy."

"Oh! Well, in that case, maybe I need a couple more pairs, Master!"

"Maybe you do." Before I can get up out of the bed, he presses me down, pins me by my shoulders, and looks down into my face. "We'll eat while we're out and when we get back, I plan to fuck you in the back yard. What do you say to that, sub?"

"Neighbors?"

"Yeah, we can invite them if you want." He grins.

"No! I mean, won't your neighbors complain, Sir?"

"They're not home during the day. We'll be alone. Unless one of them is playing hooky, and then they could get a worse show, don't you think?" He leans down and kisses me. His lips lock with mine and I'm lost in their warmth and softness. When he rises back up, I reach up and kiss him, just a peck. One hand comes up and strokes the side of my face. "You're really something, know that?"

"Yeah, but what?" I laugh.

"A bratty sub! You'd better get in that shower, bratty sub, or I'll have to spank your ass!" I wiggle out from under him and head for the shower. As I run I hear him say, "And a fine ass it is too."

I wish I hadn't heard that. Now I only want him more.

He rolls off me and onto his back in the sunlight. I'm in the shade of a small tree, and he scoots over so he's in the shade too. His arm stretches out and I pull myself to him, curling against his side, waiting for an arm to wrap around me. It does. I'm naked in his back yard on a quilt and I feel completely safe. When I kiss his chest, he pulls my face up and kisses my mouth. My arm stretches across his chest and around him and, before I know what's happening, he's rolled to face me and his cock slides into my slit, still slick and ready from the previous fucking. He rocks against me and I meet his rhythm, letting it soothe both of us.

As we continue to rock against each other, he takes his free hand and strokes my hair, my face, my neck, down my chest, my breasts, down my ribcage and my stomach, and stops to stroke my mons gently. The desire between us is like a vapor permeating everything, soaking into our skin, making its way into our lungs, into our very being. I'm almost lightheaded just from his pressure inside me, and every time he lets go a low, soft moan, every muscle below my waist constricts, tightening around him and making him moan even more. It feels so right, so tender and sweet, and I want to fuck him like this all afternoon and on into the night. "Oh, god, Master, it's so good."

"I know. You're such a joy to make love to, Trish. I don't want to stop." *Oh my god, those are almost my own words spoken back to me!*, I think, remembering when I'd said them to him. He leans in and kisses me, and I'm lost in that kiss, melting into him, wanting him, needing him.

"Oh, god, Clint, your cock is so powerful." The minute the words are out of my mouth, he shoves a palm behind my head and pulls my mouth to his, kissing me hard and long, his tongue exploring everywhere, thrashing against my tongue, drinking me in, and I let him. I let his passion pour into me, down deep and strong, and wish for more, long for more.

When he pulls back, he kisses my forehead, eyes, cheeks, nose, chin, and then plants another one on my lips. This one is soft and gentle, like a whisper, and I hold very still to enjoy it in its simplicity. Breaking the kiss, he says softly, "Hearing you say my name while I pump into you sets me on fire, Vännan. I can't get enough." He kisses me again and my arms wind around his neck, where they stay for at least another hour as we press our bodies together and come over and over.

This is what I was looking for. I want to bond with Clint Winstead. But I'm still not sure he wants to bond with me.

Tuesday morning is beautiful. He wanted me in his bed all night, and now I'm sucking cock like a maniac. He's groaning and thrusting his hips and I'm excited just watching how excited he is. I take it down deep and with the third drop he cries out, "Oh, god, Vännan, your mouth is so damn good. Suck me, baby! Oh, yeah . . . oh my god, harder, babe. Suck it harder, babe, oh god." I wish I could smile around the big, rigid thing, because I really, really want to.

He takes my head in his hands and starts to pound into my throat, and I take it, my nose and eyes running, letting him use my mouth the same way he uses my pussy and my ass, crazy and frantic and deep. Huge and steely, it gets harder still, and I know he's getting ready to fill my throat. "Oh, god, Vännan, I'm coming. Suck it down, baby, drink it." He floods my throat, my mouth, choking me, drowning me, and once I've finally managed to swallow it all, I start licking his shaft like a lollipop, circling the head with my tongue, making him moan and shake. He pops up onto his knees, pulls me up against him, and kisses me, working to taste himself in my mouth, and I share freely.

"Good, Master?" I pant when he pulls back and rests his forehead against mine.

"Oh, little sub, yeah. You're good, very, very good." He grins at me. "I've got a surprise for you later. It will be very *not* vanilla. I'll expect you to follow protocol to the letter."

"What, Master? Tell me!" I cry out, tickling his ribs and making him squirm.

"No! It won't be a surprise if I tell you now. But be assured, it's pretty spectacular. Let's eat some breakfast."

"Can I get out of your bed, Master?" I ask sarcastically.

"No. You're trapped here," he laughs and tickles me back. I shriek. "Get your ass into the bathroom and get cleaned up, missy, and do your anal prep while you're at it. Then get to the kitchen – I'm hungry." He heads off to his bathroom and I watch his fine, fine ass retreating across the room. He calls back, "Are you staring at my ass?"

"Me, Master? Why would you think that?" I giggle.

"No reason. Except I'd be staring at yours if it was the other way around. So I just assumed . . ."

"Not conceited, are you, Master?" I laugh.

He laughs back. "Nope. Just convinced."

I wander down the hallway to my bathroom. I hope this surprise is a good one.

Just as I start to step into the shower, my cell rings: Ron. "What the fuck do you want?" I snarl into it when I answer.

"Where the hell are you? I've been over here four days in a row and can't catch you at home." He sounds like he's eating something. My food, I'm sure.

"None of your damn business."

"Some little old ladies' crocheting circle? Tea with the girls? Shopping for lingerie at the granny panty store?" he laughs.

I'll show you, motherfucker. "I'm at a man's house. Having an adventure." I wait. He doesn't disappoint.

"A man? What man?"

I'm working hard to keep from laughing. "A man I just met a while back. I'm staying with him for two weeks." I think about it for only a nanosecond before I say, "I'm getting ready to take a shower. I just sucked his cock for about, oh, forty-five minutes. I'm surprisingly good at it."

I hear this choking sound. "You did what? For forty-five minutes?"

"Yeah, you heard me." Now I'm really having to fight to keep from laughing. "His is big and hard. Makes yours look like a seventh-grader's."

"And I guess you're having sex with him?" he asks, and I can tell he doesn't believe me.

"Actually, I am. In the back yard. Oh, yeah, and yesterday he double penetrated me with his dick and a huge dildo. And I liked it. He taught me to do anal prep so I'll be clean as a whistle when he wants to fuck my ass." I hear an honest-to-god choking sound now. "And the other day he took me on a hike, and when we got to the edge of the lake, he told me to get undressed and get down on my knees and suck him. Then he fucked me on a giant rock, right there in the open, and three hikers came along and watched him fuck me. It was very exciting."

Then I hear him snicker. "Oh, is that right? That's quite a story, Trish. So this guy is some kind of sex god?"

"Yes. And I'm a sex goddess. And you can believe me or you don't have to." I can tell he doesn't believe me at all.

I hear a sound behind me and turn to see Clint standing in the doorway, and he's grinning from ear to ear. He points to the phone, then to his ring finger, and I nod. Next thing I know, he's standing behind me, his arms wrapped around my waist, and he says, so close to the phone that Ron can hear, "Hey, baby, hurry up and get your shower and I'll fuck you in the back seat of the car. Whaddya say?"

I whisper back loudly enough for Ron to hear, "Oooooo, sounds delicious! But would you fuck me in the shower first? I've never done that. My old man was sooooo boring." Clint makes a big production out of kissing me with enough "smack" that Ron's sure to be able to hear.

There's silence, and then Ron asks, "Trish, who is that?"

"None of your goddamn business, asshole." Clint kisses the side of my neck and I giggle.

"Who's on the phone, princess? My cock is lonely for that hot, wet, tight little cunt of yours. Hang up so we can get on with the fuckathon, please?" I turn to look into Clint's face and he looks like a naughty little boy, a huge grin stretching his lips, so big that his eyes are squeezed shut. It's all I can do to keep from laughing right out loud. The playful side of him is poking out all over.

"Ron, I've got to go. What I've got going on here is far more interesting than this dreary conversation. I told you before, you take anything of mine and I'll hunt your sorry ass down. Now leave me alone." I hit end before he can say anything else, and Clint roars with laughter.

"Thanks, Master! Thanks for playing along. You have no idea how good that felt," I grin and kiss him.

"Wow – I'm a sex god. Who knew?" he laughs.

"You know that already. You're my sex god, Master," I grin and kiss his cheek.

"And you're my cock-sucking, all-night-fucking sex goddess, Vännan!" he chuckles. "Was that who I think it was?"

"Yes. And we gave him something to think about for awhile," I chuckle.

"Is this your way of getting back at him? Will you take him back?" Out of nowhere, Clint sobers. There's something sad on his face.

I stroke his cheek. "No, Master. I'm done with him. I'm looking for something far more exciting."

"Then get done with your shower and I'll bring your search to an end, sub." He kisses me hard, then turns me toward the shower and slaps the cheek of my ass as he leaves the room.

I do a little heart check. Yeah, it's official.

I'm in love with Clint Winstead.

I'm sitting in the living room, making notes in my journal, when he walks in, magnificently naked. His huge, purple rod is standing at attention, bobbing with its own pulse, and I want it to have *my* attention. It's a beautiful thing.

"I'm hard and ready for you, Vännan. Your body is my plaything. Are you ready to please me?" The formality of this scene is more than edgy; this is the moment when he stops being Clint or Sir and becomes my Master. I keep my eyes down and nod breathlessly, so turned on that I'm almost twitching all over. "I want you to remain silent throughout this experience. Not a sound." There's a part of me that's glad I'm ordered into silence because I'm so aroused that if I could speak, I would probably humiliate myself.

He motions for me to follow, then turns and strolls into his bathroom with me right behind him; that ass is perfection, and I'm getting wet just watching him walk in front of me. His shower stall is huge, lined with dark tile and adorned with metallic accents, and it has an enormous bench built into the back wall. Placed on the bench is a medium-sized storage tub. He opens the wide, tempered-glass door and motions for me to follow. Ah, sex in the shower, just like I asked. This'll be good.

When I join him in his tiled sanctuary, he spreads a large, plush towel on the bench and takes a seat. His enormous manhood is still vibrating with its own pulse, a pearly drop of pre-cum greeting me on its velvety head.

"Turn with your back to me." I don't waste any time doing so. "Hands on the floor." I bend and place my hands as far onto the floor as I can manage. There's a snap of a bottle cap, and in a few seconds, cold lube drips down the crack of my ass. I hear the bottle snap shut, and then he starts to rim my anus with his finger. He pumps a finger in and out of me, then two. After a minute or so, he replaces the two with three and I almost moan; it's hard not to. I feel him try to spread the three fingers apart and the stretch that accompanies his effort. The burn is fearsome and delicious.

Then he pulls his fingers out. "Nice and tight." He stands and grips my hip with one hand. I can feel his cock head against my tiny hole, and then he's pressing in. The only way I can keep silent is to bite my lip, which I do – hard. He sinks into me slowly, but then his work takes a forceful turn, and the pressure and pain are intense as he forces his way through my ring of muscles. "I've used your ass over and over, but you're still tight like an anal virgin. Amazing." His words come out almost as a groan, and they snatch the breath from my lungs. "You use red as your safeword, correct?" When I nod again, he pulls back, then rams into my ass.

I fight to keep my voice paralyzed. He draws back out and plows in again, striking deep inside my constriction, both hands gripping my hips. A tear escapes my eye, but I hold firm. When he's completely in me up to his balls, he whispers, "Stand up." His arms go around my waist and he takes one step backward, then sits down on the bench with me firmly impaled on his shaft.

The pain ignites my desire, and my clit's begun a vicious, relentless throbbing. I wonder if he's going to want me to ride his magnificence. Instead, he grips my thighs from underneath, lifts my legs, and drops them back onto his with my calves on the outsides of his legs. It dawns on me that he can butterfly my legs completely open by moving his apart. He opens the storage tub, but when I try to look, he snaps, "Eyes to the front! This is about trust. Do you trust me?" I nod. I can hear him moving things around.

He leans slightly forward and draws something around my chest above my breasts – a wide nylon strap with a buckle. Once he's fastened it, he tightens it, and that's when I understand; it wraps around both of us. He's bound me to him, my back to his chest. When he leans forward the second time, another strap appears around my waist. I'm bound to him in a way that leaves me completely unable to move independently. Two more straps go around our thighs, as far up as he can get them, and another pair just above our knees.

"Put your wrists together." When I get them crossed, he ties them with a length of nylon rope, leaving two long tails. "Over your head and behind it." I bring my arms up and drop my hands behind my head, and he slips his head into the circle of my arms. Then he takes the rope ends and brings them around in front of us, tying them together. That's it – I can't move without his help.

This binding is erotic in a way I've never experienced. I am, for all intents and purposes, one with him, completely at his mercy. His cock is deep inside my back channel, and I can't move unless he does, so it's pretty clear he won't be pumping into me with his dick. The helplessness I feel sends white-hot current from my scalp to the soles of my feet, but I can't figure out what he's about to do.

Reaching around both of us, he parts my labial lips and presses a finger into my pussy. "You're already wet. Good. I suppose you're curious about what I'm going to do with you." I nod, and he draws the finger up inside my slit until he finds my clit, circling it ever so gently. "You'll like it. You'll beg for it again before the week is over. It will satisfy you in a way you've never known before." His certainty makes me shiver. But I can't help wondering: If he's just going to finger me, why in the shower?

Master leans us both forward and starts the water in the shower. It doesn't come out of the shower head up on the wall; instead, it shoots out of a hand-held shower head lower, below the control. After waiting for the water to warm up, he takes the hand-held head and trains the water on my mons. "Too hot?" I shake my head.

Oh my god. As I understand what he's planning to do, a painful thrumming sets up just behind my nub. He turns a ring on the shower head, and I watch in horror and fascination as the water goes from a rain-like circle to a pulsing, concentrated stream. Something deep inside me makes me wish I was wearing a blindfold.

"I see you understand what I'm about to do. I will take you somewhere you'll want to go over and over. And you will be completely silent, do you understand?" I nod. "Not a peep. Again, safeword – you may speak."

"Red, Master."

"Very good. Prepare yourself." He places his finger over my clit and moves the showerhead. When he takes his finger away, the stream is shooting directly into my swollen little nodule.

No doubt about it, it's beyond stimulating. I can barely wait to feel the orgasm building, to feel the pressure mounting, to come, unable to thrust my hips or close my legs because of our bindings and the way his legs hold mine open. I can feel myself slipping into it, the clenching and releasing deep in my core, and I'm ready for it.

Before I can fall into it, he reaches back into the plastic tub and pulls out a giant dildo, bigger than the one he used when he double penetrated me. He places it at the entrance to my pussy and pushes it into my already-slick channel. It fills me up to bursting with his cock in my ass, and I fight the urge to cry out.

Holding the dildo in place with his free hand, his fingers trail up my slit to my clit once more. But this time he surprises me. He spreads our legs wider, then uses his index finger to retract the hood over my pearl and hold it. With his middle finger placed directly over my bud, he shifts us ever so slightly and then removes the second finger.

It's blinding. A jetted stream of water hits my plumped-up, fully-exposed clit full force, and I fight to keep from gasping. I can't move, can't escape, can't even draw my legs together, and I can't remember my safeword, even though it's just about as standard as they come. All I can do is feel the pain of the concentrated stream of water drilling into the most sensitive spot on my body, spiking into it, and the knotting of the muscles in my abdomen and pussy are going from rippling to excruciating spasms in a matter of seconds. I want him to stop, but I also desperately want it, what he's offering me, the pain and the release, so many sensations bombarding me that I fight to keep my wits about me. More than anything, I want him to be pleased with me and enjoy me. I want him to want me more than he's ever wanted any woman. I can barely breathe, and I know that, whatever my body does, it will be violent. It's a struggle to stay quiet.

"So intense. So painful. So hungry for it," he whispers, and a wild shudder runs through the deepest part of me as his breath tickles my ear. I almost whimper, but I want more than anything to follow his orders and stay silent, to please him and to show him that I can take whatever he challenges me with. Everything is building, the spasms in my gut almost unbearable, and then it happens.

I come. The orgasm swallows me whole, dropping me into a darkness that has no bottom. Every inch of my body is sizzling, my hips unable to churn, my legs spread so wide that there's no escape. No muscle in my being is relaxed; everything is drawn up and screaming. My hands fight against his neck and the rope, and my body struggles to be released from the straps, but there's no release and no relief. A silent scream forms on my lips, and I can feel my eyes rolling back, but there's nothing I can do as my body goes into complete overload and I lose any control I might've had. My head thrashes. My legs cramp. And he keeps going, never letting up, never moving the stream of water, and it's too much. I hear myself make a guttural sound followed by a shriek the likes of which I've never uttered before. That's all I remember.

When I manage to pry an eye open, I look around. I'm in Master's bed, naked and wet, but stretched out and comfortable with a sheet drawn over me. There's soft music playing, some kind of jazz. As I listen, I can hear his voice somewhere in the house.

"Yeah. And I'm worried. She still hasn't come around . . . I tried that. This has never happened before, and there's no way for me to know if . . . Do you think I should call an ambulance? Her pulse is strong and her breathing is even." I can hear his voice getting closer, and then it's in the room. "She's awake. Gotta go." Before I can say or do anything, he's there, his arms wrapping around me, pulling me against his body.

"Jesus, are you okay?" I shrug – I'm not sure, because I can't figure out what happened. "You scared me to death." Because I'm pretty sure I'm not supposed to speak, I just bury my face in his chest.

"Hey. We need to go vanilla now," he says, pulling my face up so I can look into his. There's worry in those sweet eyes. "I want you to talk to me. Trish, baby, what happened in there?"

I shake my head. "I don't know. One minute I was in the shower with you. The next, I was waking up in here."

"You passed out cold. That's never happened before." He strokes my face as he speaks.

"So you do this with subs often?"

"Just occasionally."

"And this has never happened before?" I'm having trouble believing that. How could anyone take anything that intense?

"No. There's a really good reason for that too." He draws my face up and looks directly into my eyes. "No other sub has ever let that happen. They safeworded the split second the orgasm hit. You're the first sub I've done that with who's hung in there and ridden the crest. I saw things in there with you that I've never seen before. Frankly, I probably would've stopped a lot sooner, but I was so caught up in watching you, your body, the way you were responding, that I forgot to turn off the water." He kisses me gently, then puts his hand under my chin to hold my gaze. "You wanted it. You wanted whatever I gave you. You were determined to say nothing, to follow my orders, to take it. You wanted me to own your body."

I can feel my face starting to burn. I'd wanted it so badly, to please him, to know if he came inside me as I writhed, that I hadn't given a thought to myself. Well, if he had come inside me, I missed it. Apparently I missed quite a few things, unconscious as I was. I'm sure my cheeks are flaming in embarrassment.

"Why are you blushing?" There's no way I'm meeting his eyes. "Why would you be embarrassed?"

"I'm afraid of what you must think of me," I whisper.

"What do you mean? What do you *think* I think of you?" he quizzes, a puzzled look on his face.

I can't look at him. "You must think I'm the biggest slut you've ever seen." There's a tear threatening to roll down my cheek, and I decide if that happens, if I cry, I'll just have to leave. I wouldn't be able to take any more from him. All I'd wanted was to make him happy with me.

"Baby, that was the most incredible thing I've ever seen." I think for a second that I've heard him wrong, and my eyes rotate straight toward his. "I've never seen a woman just lose herself in an orgasm to the point of unconsciousness. I won't lie – you scared the shit out of me, and I'm not eager to experience that again. But it was, well, it was just fucking amazing, angel. It made me feel like the most powerful man on earth, knowing you were satisfied in a way I've never satisfied any other woman." He kisses my forehead. "I need to tell you something."

"Yes, Master?"

"I got a chance to peek into the envelopes before we left the club the other day." He'd peeked too? I can't believe it. "And I know what was in them."

I nod. "I peeked too."

"No! Really? So you know too?" He seems completely at a loss. "What do you make of it? I'd just like to hear your opinion."

I shrug. "I don't know. But if I had to guess, I'd say Dave thought we should do this together. I don't know why. Do you?"

He smiles. "I have no idea why. But right now," he says, kissing the tip of my nose, "I'd say Dave is a very wise man." He closes his eyes and sighs. "I would've been devastated if you'd gone with anyone else," he adds, and I know he means Master Steffen.

Clint wanted me. He wanted to spend these weeks with me. And we wound up together. There's a tiny little hint of fear on his face when he asks, "Were you disappointed? Did you want to go with . . . someone else?"

I shake my head, and I'm not lying. "I was relieved, even glad, when they called my name with yours. I was afraid, but I was glad too. You were the one I wanted to go with, Master." I can't believe I just admitted that, but it feels good to get the words out into the air.

"Vanilla. Call me by my name – call me by my name, Trish. I need to hear it." He bends to my neck and starts to kiss it.

"I'm glad they called my name with yours, Clint." His head snaps up and he crushes his lips to mine, his tongue parting them and our tongues dancing together. That's when I feel it. Something powerful is going on between us, something I can't identify because I've never felt anything like it, like a magnetic current holding us together, my lips tingling as they press to his. He breaks the kiss but, before I can say anything, he pulls back and looks into my face.

"Trish, I probably shouldn't say this, but . . . no, I can't." *Oh, god*, I think, *please tell me you feel something for me.*

"What," I ask, then add, "Clint?" The minute his name hits the air again, his lips return, urgent and demanding, his hands cupping my breasts, drifting downward, and resting on the tops of my hips. I think since he didn't finish the sentence, I'll feel a disconnect. It's anything but.

Then he stops. "Feel okay?" I nod. "Let's get cleaned up, get dressed, go out. I'll take you to dinner. I'll call some friends, see if they can meet us. How does that sound?" He smiles at me and taps his fingertip on the end of my nose.

"What will you tell them? How will you explain me? Will you tell them I'm your sub?"

He laughs. "Nope. Vanilla, baby. I'll just tell them you're my date."

"By the way," I say and look into his eyes, "can we do that again?"

His mouth drops open, and then he says, "Are you serious? You've got to be either brave or crazy, girl."

"Yes," I grin. "I am." Brave or crazy – there's a difference?

There are two guys, Matt and Adam, and their girlfriends, Sarah and Amy, respectively. The guys are friends from the place where Clint used to work. We meet them at a bar and grill downtown a couple of blocks from the club. The guys seem nice enough. The girlfriends eye me suspiciously. I can tell they're wondering about me, I assume about the age difference between Clint and me. I know I look good for my age, but I *am* still almost fifty. I'm under no illusion here.

"So, where did you two meet?" Matt asks.

Clint takes another sip of his whiskey. "At a club here in town."

"Funny, you don't look like the kind that would go 'clubbing,'" Sarah snarks toward me, using air quotes. I see Clint shoot me a look. He's wondering how I'll respond.

I think back to what Dave taught me: *A sub's behavior and demeanor reflect on her master.* "Looks can be deceiving," I say smartly and look back down into my drink. Cosmo. He remembered.

"Not that kind of club. Book club. We were reading, what was that book?" he asks, smiling at me. Little shit.

"I think it was a Barbara Kingsolver. No, maybe Amy Tan." Now I'm smiling and he's scrambling.

"I've never read an Amy Tan in my life," he throws back, and I start laughing.

"I'm just kidding. I don't remember what the book was. I was too busy looking at the scenery," I say and blush. I feel his hand on my leg, and he squeezes it just above my knee. Everything between my legs ignites.

We eat huge burgers and homemade potato chips, and we ask for water when we've finished our drinks. I excuse myself and leave to go to the restroom. When I come out of the stall, Amy is standing there in front of the sink, preening in the mirror. "So, when did you and Clint start going out?"

"We've only been seeing each other a couple of weeks," I offer. Well, it's true. A week and a half.

"Oh. Have you met the girls?" She's putting on fresh blush.

"No. They're visiting his mother right now." I check my eye makeup – still looks fine.

"Oh. Shame about his wife, huh?" She's not looking at me at all, so fortunately she can't try to read my face. She wouldn't like what she'd see on it.

"Yes, it is." I have no idea what she's talking about. He's never shared any of this with me, but I don't want her to know that.

"He's had a very hard time since, well, you know." She puts on more lip liner. "We've never seen him with a woman since then. But I guess you know all about that."

As much as I want to ask what happened, my irritation turns to an overwhelming anger. This is my Master she's talking about. She's trying to divulge *his* personal information, discussing it like it was coffee chat. And I find that even though I'm curious, I hate that. I just reply, "That's Clint's personal business. I don't feel free to discuss that."

She spins and stares at me, eyebrows peaking. "Really? Hmmm. That's a new one. So much for getting to know you." She turns and stomps out of the restroom. Getting to know me? She wasn't trying to get to know me. She wanted me to betray my Master, and I wouldn't. I want to run out there and tell him, but I'll wait until we leave.

The girlfriends say nothing to me for the rest of the evening. At eleven, Clint says, "I think we need to get going. Morning's going to come fast." We get up from the table and make all the appropriate goodbyes. The girls are very stand-offish to me, but the guys are warm and friendly. I'm careful to do nothing that would look like flirting.

We walk back to the car hand in hand. "That didn't go very well, did it?" he suddenly asks.

I shrug. "I guess not."

"Why, do you think?" he asks me, and I can tell from his tone that he's sincere, not angry.

I can't look up at him. "The girlfriends didn't like me. First, they thought I was too old for you. I think when they asked where we met, they expected you to tell them that you met me when you were volunteering at the nursing home where I live." Clint roars with laughter. "I'm not kidding," I almost whisper, and he quiets.

"Sorry. I guess that isn't funny, but . . ." and he starts laughing again. I lay a silly slap on his shoulder. "I'm sorry, I'm sorry! Okay. Anything else?"

"Yes." I don't know how to tell him this. "When I was in the restroom, Amy was in there."

"Yeah?"

"She was asking me questions and making comments about you and . . . your wife." I know he doesn't want to talk about this.

He doesn't look upset or angry, just curious. "Not surprising. What did she say?"

"Not much. She kept saying, 'You know, with all he's been through,' and 'But I'm sure you know more than we do,' and things like that." I stop. It hurts me to know that he hasn't trusted me enough to tell me anything, that casual acquaintances know more about him than I do.

"Did that bother you?" His voice is quiet and serious.

"A little. But what bothered me more was that she was willing to break your confidence like that. I decided I didn't like her talking about my Master that way. That's hurtful." I'm trying to turn loose of his hand, but he's gripping mine tighter. He stops on the sidewalk.

"Trish?" I can't look up at him. "Trish, look at me." My face is red and my eyes are tearing up. "Sub, obey me." I know he can see the reluctance on my face as I look up into his eyes. "I need to tell you thanks. Most women would've jumped right in, picked and poked, asked lots of questions. You didn't. I appreciate that." I try to turn away again, but he grips my chin in his hand and turns my face to his, locking his eyes with mine. "Do you trust me to tell you when it's time? To know when to tell you? So that I know you're ready to hear it?"

I nod. "Yes, Master. I trust you."

He smiles. "Very good. That's all I ask. And thanks again for your protection. You have no idea what that means to me." He kisses my lips lightly, then takes my hand and we stroll to the car in silence.

Chapter 10

He was right. I've started to enjoy the taste of his cum in my coffee. It's still in my mouth when I take the first big sip, and it's heaven. I'm not about to tell him he was right, though. Some things are better left unsaid.

I've treated him to my famous farmhouse omelet. There's very little in the kitchen that didn't make its way into the beautiful egg dish. We eat and laugh and talk about what we did when we got home the night before. He tied my hands to the headboard and tortured my pussy with his tongue until I was screaming, then fucked me hard and fast while I begged him for more. And that was just the warm-up.

We've both had showers, gotten dressed, and he's thinking about taking me to a movie when his cell phone rings. I'm looking on my tablet at the movie times when he answers it and says, "Hi!" Almost instantly his face changes. "What? Where? I'm on my way!" He hits end and yells, "Stay here! I'll call as soon as I can."

"Sir, what's going on?" I can tell that he's frantic and it's scaring me as he scrambles around to get only what he needs.

"My oldest fell. They think she's broken her wrist. I've got to get to the hospital. I'll be back as soon as I can."

"Please be . . ." I'm calling out as he closes the door. ". . . careful." But he's already gone.

I settle back into the sofa with my cell in my pocket so I'll know if it rings and can answer it when he calls. I hope the little girl's all right, and then I realize I don't even know her name. I go to the mantel and take down a photo of the two girls, open the back of the frame, and look at the back of the photo. There are two names written there; "Hailee, 10, McKenna, 8." So the hospital trip must be Hailee. I return it to the mantel carefully and sit back down to wait.

When the house phone rings I almost jump out of my skin. It hasn't rung since I've been here, so it startles me at first, and when I realize what it is, I bolt to answer it.

"Hello?" I say, gasping for breath.

"Hello. I'd like to speak with Clint Winstead. Is he available?" a man's voice asks.

"No, sir, I'm sorry, he's out. May I take a message?" I grab a pad of paper and look around – nothing to write with.

"No, ma'am. I've tried to call his cell but he's not answering. Maybe you can help me. I'm one of Mr. Winstead's clients, and I'm in the middle of a meeting. I can't seem to find my copy of his proposal. Could you look it up for me and fax me a copy?"

"Well, sir, I'm just a friend. He had a family emergency. I really don't know . . ."

"It's the Cumberland Mission School. Not hard to find. It's about three pages. Could you just look around for me? I've got to present this to the board and I need it immediately."

Crap. I have no idea what to do. His messenger bag is behind the chair, so I pull it out and go through the papers in it – nothing. "Sir, could you hang on? It's not in his bag. Let me go look somewhere else."

"Certainly. No problem."

"Thanks." I head down the hall and then freeze. He told me the office was off limits. But this man is in a meeting, trying to bring Clint's proposal to the table before his board of directors. Clint could lose this job if I don't find the proposal for the man on the phone. I'm satisfied that he'd want me to do this, so I open the door and peek inside.

It just looks like your regular home office. Books and papers are everywhere. I see a stack of things that look like proposals, spreadsheet-like stuff, and I turn on the ceiling light and start looking through them. Sure enough, three proposals down there's one that says, "Tom Norsworthy, Cumberland Mission School." I grab it and run back up the hall, then remember to grab a pencil.

"Yes, hello, sorry about that." I'm breathless. "Sir, your name, would it be Tom . . ."

"Norsworthy."

"Yes! I found it. Can you give me your fax number? I'll fax it right over." He recites it to me; I write it down, then repeat it, and we hang up. I go back to the office and find the fax machine, put the proposal on it, and start punching buttons. In just a couple of minutes I've sent the proposal and generated a fax receipt showing that it was sent. That gets paper-clipped to the proposal and returned to the stack.

As I leave the room I close the door, and I feel pretty good about what I just did. I saved the day. He shouldn't have to worry about anything except his little girl. Then I realize: She's going to want to come home with him. And he's going to want me to leave.

I don't know what to do. I don't want to leave, but I understand his need to protect his children. Then I laugh. Protect them from me. That's kind of funny, really, the woman who always wanted children but her husband didn't.

I go back to the living room, pull out my reader, and start reading an ebook I bought the week before. It's pretty good, and I'm engrossed when I hear his car alarm. I drop the tablet and kneel in my spot.

The door opens and Clint comes in, looking kind of frazzled. I keep my eyes down and wait. He crosses to me and puts his hand on my head, and I can't help but blurt out, "I'm sorry, Master, but I'm so concerned. Is everything all right?"

He sighs, sits down on the sofa, and motions for me to join him. When I start to sit down, once again he pulls me onto his lap and cuddles me to him. "Yeah. She's fine. Just a sprain. Didn't even want to come home. My mother promised the girls she'd take them to the zoo tomorrow, so she wants to stay there." *Good. At least that worry's gone*, I think. "Anything interesting happen around here while I was gone?"

I tremble a little as I start to tell him. "Well, this man called, Tom Norsworthy? He said he's a client of yours." Clint nods. "I asked if I could take a message, but he said no. He told me he was in a board meeting at that very minute and he couldn't find the proposal you'd brought to him. He had to pitch it to the board to get it approved. I told him there was nothing I could do, but he insisted I go and look for it." I keep my fingers crossed in my mind.

A look passes over Clint's face, one I don't recognize. "And what did you do?"

Now I'm scared. "He just insisted that he had to have it, so I went in and found it. He wanted it faxed to him, so I faxed it to him and printed a fax receipt for you." The look that's growing on his face is something that's chilling me. "Then I put everything back and closed the door immediately. I didn't look around or anything, really, just that. That's all, Master, I swear."

He doesn't speak for about three minutes or so. Then he says, "I told you the office was off limits to you, did I not?"

Now I'm shaking. "Yes, Master, you did, but I didn't want you to lose the deal. He wouldn't take no for an answer, and I just thought . . ."

He pushes me off his lap and stands, then turns, his eyes burning into me. "I didn't bring you here to think. I brought you here to serve me. And this is how you repay me?"

My eyes fly open wide. "I was doing you a favor, Master! I helped. I *am* serving you."

His face goes dark and I shudder. "You openly defied me. And you will be punished."

"But Master, I . . ."

"No buts. You broke protocol. And you broke my trust. As far as I'm concerned, that's even worse. I can make you keep protocol, but I can't make you trustworthy. And I obviously can't trust you." The fury in his voice makes my stomach quiver.

"Master, I didn't do it to defy you. I did it to help. Please . . . I just wanted to do the right thing, so I had to think about it, what you would want me to do, and I thought you'd want me to, I don't know, get something so . . ." I'm babbling now.

"Silence!" he yells, and I go quiet. I don't know what's going to happen. He paces back and forth for a minute, then he turns to me, or maybe I should say turns *on* me. "That was the only thing I was rigid about, the only thing. And you defied me." I start to say something, but he barks, "I don't care about the proposal or the fax machine or any of that. It wasn't about the room. It was about whether or not I can trust you, and I obviously can't."

I whisper so low that I'm sure he can't hear, "But he didn't want to leave a message." And that's it. I can't take it anymore. I feel a tear roll down one cheek, and another one tries to escape down the other. I can't stop them. I feel sick, I'm exhausted, I hurt from kneeling so much, and I don't know what to do to please him. I stare at the floor and wish I were anywhere else but here.

"I'm going out. I'll be gone for thirty minutes. Have an early dinner ready when I come back. Then you'll receive your punishment." With that, he storms out the door and I'm left there alone.

I put water on to boil and then throw pasta into it. In a couple of minutes I realize that I should've waited until the sauce was hot, but I don't care. I open the jar, pour it into the saucepan, add the veggies and mushrooms, and turn it on to heat.

As I stand there, I think about what just happened. He can't trust me. Why? All I did was try to save his ass. Yes, I know he told me not to go in there, but he also told me to take messages for phone calls, and the man didn't want to leave a message; the guy was in a jam, and I did what needed to be done. It could've been a situation where not finding that and faxing it cost Clint the whole deal. My main thought was to preserve his success. And I got yelled at for caring – yay me.

My back is turned to the door when he comes in, and I pretend I don't hear him. I'm not going to the door and kneel only to get yelled at again. He doesn't speak to me, just stalks off down the hallway. In a little while, he comes back into the kitchen. His voice is flat when he asks, "Is the food ready?"

"Yes, Sir. Shall I serve you, Sir?" I ask, and I wonder if he can see me shiver.

"Yes." That's all he says. I get a plate, put some pasta on it and spoon the sauce over it, then garnish it with some grated parmesan. I put a couple of slices of garlicky toasted French bread on the plate with it and carry it to the table. He moves his arms out of the way and I put the plate down in front of him, then move to stand about a foot behind him on his right.

"You should probably eat now. The rest of the afternoon and evening will be more unpleasant than the previous," he says in a menacing tone. I don't respond. "Well, eat, why don't you?" he almost yells.

I just stand there, fighting to hold back the tears. Finally, I whisper, "I'm not hungry, Master."

He shakes his head. "Suit yourself." I watch him eating, and then he says, "It's actually edible."

And that's when I know. This was his way of having a housekeeper, cook, and sex slave for two weeks. He's not interested in me or anything about me. I feel sad and stupid at the same time. I've got three more days and I can get away from this, this feeling of being squashed and hated and degraded by someone who vacillates between wanting me with him and wishing me gone. I know Dave thought this was a good idea, and I respect Dave and his opinion, but this time he was just plain wrong.

He eats everything on the plate, and I take it to the sink, rinse it, and put it in the dishwasher. Then I busy myself putting away the leftovers. I can feel him watching me from behind, but I don't turn around or say anything. He's not interested in anything I've got to say anyway.

When all of the work is done, I let out an involuntary sigh. He must take that as a sign that I'm ready, because he simply says, "Sub, go and lie across your bed." I go down the hall and do as he instructed. I need to pee, but I don't bother. If I wet the bed, I'm the one who'll have to lie in it for the night, so I don't really care.

"On your stomach. Hands behind your back." I do as he says, and he cuffs my wrists there, not with soft cuffs but with plain metal ones that bite into them. I don't wonder anymore what he's going to do; it doesn't matter. "Head up," he snarls, and then there's a ball gag in my mouth. I can feel him working behind me, and he's doing something with my feet. When he's done, he just says, "If your feet take you where I've told you not to go, they should be punished. At least thirty minutes." With that, he walks out.

I'm trying to figure out what he's done when I start to feel the sensation: Ice. He's bound something icy on the soles of my feet, then bound them together so I can't move them. As I lie there, horrified, the pain starts to intensify as they get colder and colder. In eight minutes, it's almost unbearable, and I've got twenty-two more to endure.

I don't know if it's the lack of food or my nerves, but the wave of nausea slams into me and I start to heave. There's nothing in there, so it's just dry heaves, my stomach trying to empty itself of something that's not there because the pain is so intense. It's good I didn't eat anything or I would aspirate. Worse yet, I know he doesn't care, and I can't safeword with a gag in my mouth, so I just lie there as it goes on and on. Sometime during that period of time my bladder turns loose, and I feel the heat and wetness spreading underneath me, but I say nothing. Even if I could, there's no point.

Nothing I could say would change his mind, make him like me, make him care. Nothing. He said in Dave's office that day that he really does care about me, but it appears he said that solely for Dave's benefit. I think about what Steffen said to me that first night I scened at the club, about a Dom's responsibility being to take care of the sub and look out for her wellbeing, and I realize that Clint isn't a very good Dom. He's got some point to make, and I'm the pad he's writing it on. And when he's finished, he'll just erase it all, then tear me off, wad me up, and throw me away like I was never here. Like I'm not important, like my feelings don't matter. The pain in my feet is so bad that my mind has started to shut down, and I choke and sputter behind the gag as my stomach continues to heave. Through it all, he doesn't even come to check on me.

I don't know how long it's been, but something happens to me. I feel weird, disoriented, disconnected, like something strange is happening to my body, and parts of it jerk and twist independent of my control. It's a sort of floating feeling, and I'm no longer in any kind of pain. I hear what sounds like a door opening, but it sounds far, far away, and then someone is taking the cuffs off my wrists. I hear a voice, but it's distant. Then there's a loud buzzing sound like a billion cicadas in my head, and someone is saying, "Trish! Trish, are you okay? Trish?" My face is being slapped and I can't make sense of anything. It gets quiet again, and then there's a cool cloth on my face, wiping it, and when I can get my wits about me, I see Clint sitting on the bed beside me, a strange, frightened look on his face. "Trish? Talk to me! Trish?"

I'm trying to make words, but I can't. There's a funny feeling in my face, like it's frozen or paralyzed, kind of tingly and tight. When I do manage, all I can think to say is, "You're sitting in my pee."

"Trish, you were supposed to tell me all of your medical history. You should've told me you have seizures."

I shake my head. "I've never had a seizure in my life. I don't know what you're talking about." In that instant, I'm overcome with exhaustion. I can't even raise my head, and my mouth, dry as the Sahara, won't work to say anything else. When my eyes close, I'm thankful, and I give in to the drowsiness.

The room is dark when I wake up, and I'm somewhere else – Clint's bed? I can hear movement in the house, but I can't tell what or from where. Then Clint walks past the door with the sheets from my bed all bundled up in his arms, so I guess he's trying to get everything cleaned up. I'm fairly certain he won't want me in his bed all night. Maybe he's going to sleep in there. I really don't care. I don't have enough energy to do anything, so he can do whatever he wants. Besides, he's going to anyway. He closes the door before he goes on up the hallway.

My mouth is so sticky and dry that I can hardly move my tongue. I guess he notices that my eyes were open before, because he opens the door, sticks his head in, and then comes in. The lamp snaps on, low beam, and he sits down on the side of the bed. I can't read his expression. Maybe he's worried; if he is, it's just because he'll be held responsible if something happens to me. He sure as hell doesn't care about my welfare.

"Trish, are you okay? What happened? It looked like you were having a seizure. Do you remember what happened?"

All I can do is shake my head. My tongue is so swollen that I can't talk. "Can you tell me what happened?" he asks again. I shake my head once more. He gets up, leaves, and comes back with a glass of water. "Sit up and drink some of this." I just lie there. "Please?" I try, but I just can't get up. He moves in, wraps his arm around me, and sits me up. "Here. Please?" He puts the glass to my lips and pours a little in, and I manage to swallow.

"Feel better?" I shake my head again. All I want is to lie down and go to sleep. That must be pretty plain, because he says, "You need some rest. I'll be back in a few minutes after I lock up."

I just lie there, wondering what to do next. In a few minutes he comes back, and I hear him moving around, probably getting undressed. The bed moves and I know he's slipped in behind me. Then he moves closer and his arms encircle me.

And I scoot away. I can't help it. I just can't take it anymore. Tears spill out of my eyes and onto the pillow, and I can't breathe. I hear him quietly say, "I failed you," and then everything goes still.

When I wake up, it's light outside. I can't tell what time it is; everything is still very fuzzy. There's a smell in the house, something cooking, and I hear someone moving around. I just lie there and try to go back to sleep.

"Trish? Trish, wake up. I made you some breakfast." When I manage to pry one eye open, Clint's sitting on the side of the bed. "I know you've got to be hungry. You'll feel better if you eat. Come on, sit up." I try to push myself up, but I can't. There's a look that passes across his face – alarm? – and he helps me sort of sit up. But everything starts to move and swim and I feel dizzy and sick again. "You're getting sick because you haven't eaten. You need to eat." I shake my head. "No, really, you have to."

I manage to grunt, "Yogurt." He looks at me for a second, then disappears and comes back with a yogurt cup and a spoon.

"Here. It's," he looks at the cup, "vanilla." How ironic. "Come on, eat it. Please?" I let him spoon a couple of lumps into my mouth and manage to choke it down. And the sick feeling does seem to start going away. I open my mouth a couple more times and swallow some more. Pretty soon, the whole thing's down. He hands me a glass of water and I drink every drop. I hear something, and he says, "I'll be right back."

Before I can lie back down, I see a figure in the doorway: Dave. He walks in and sits down on the side of the bed, and I can see Clint standing in the doorway, looking worried and drawn. The first thing that runs through my mind is, *Yeah, he thinks he's in trouble.* Dave smiles down at me, but I can't smile. I don't have anything to smile about.

Dave strokes my cheek. "Trish, honey, are you okay?" I shake my head no. When I do, Clint reaches in for the doorknob and closes the door, leaving me to talk to Dave alone. "Sit up and talk to me, darlin'." When I've struggled to a full sitting position, he takes my hands. "What happened last night?"

I shake my head again – seems I'm doing that a lot lately. "I have no idea. He asked me why I didn't tell him I have a seizure disorder. I *don't* have a seizure disorder."

"Well, you had a seizure." Alarms start going off in my head. I had a seizure; he pushed me until my body revolted. Fear starts in the pit of my stomach and travels upward, but I use anger to fight back against it. "And it scared Clint to death."

"Yeah. It scared him so bad that he left me lying in there, heaving and seizing, for thirty minutes, lying in my own urine. Dave, why did you do this to me?"

He looks confused. "What do you . . ."

There's nothing left to hold back, so I just turn it all loose. "He hates me. He's hated me from the very first time he saw me, that first night at the bar when I walked down toward him and asked if the seat beside him was taken, and he just walked away. I don't know why, he just does. And you backed him into a corner, made him bring me here. I have no idea why he agreed to the pairing. I was totally shocked when he did, knowing how he feels about me. All he's done since I've been here is try to get rid of me, push me to breaking, make me feel bad about trying to serve him and follow his rules. He's set me up to fail over and over." That was something I just realized; there wasn't a damn thing wrong with what I did, and he'd admitted that there was nothing in that room that I shouldn't see. Yeah, there's someone here who shouldn't be trusted, but it isn't me. "I thought you said he was the most trustworthy person you've ever known. What the hell?"

Dave looks like I've punched him in the gut. "This is all my fault. I'm so sorry, Trish. I thought I was doing the right thing, but I think maybe Clint wasn't ready for any of this. So if you want to blame someone, blame me."

"No. He's a grown-ass man. He made his own choices." I glare at Dave. "I've got three more days. I intend to serve them if for no other reason than to prove to myself that I can. But then I'm done." I've already thought about it and if Steffen still wants me, maybe that's the direction I should go.

Dave looks down and shakes his head. "Honey, I really am sorry. I'll have a talk with Clint. I know that won't change anything, but at least . . . well, I'll talk to him. Try to get some rest, okay? And if you need me, call me." He leans in and gives me a kiss on the forehead. "But I can tell you this: If you've hung in this far, you're going to make somebody an unbelievably good sub, little one." He closes the door behind him as he leaves the room, and I'm alone again.

I don't see Clint until sometime later – I still have no concept of time – and he sticks his head in the door. "Doing okay in here?" I just nod and he closes the door again.

Sometime late afternoon I get up and half stumble, half crawl into the kitchen. Clint's sitting on the sofa, not moving, and when he sees me he half whispers, "Trish, if you need something, I'll be glad to get it for you."

Before I can stop myself, I turn and snip, "Why? Don't trust me to get into your cabinets?" I'm not sorry I said it; it actually makes me feel better. Then I get a look, a good look, at his face.

He's just staring at the floor. It's not a look that conveys a lack of caring. It's a look like he wishes he could die. I want to feel sorry for him, but I can't. I just get what I want from the cabinets, the drawers, the refrigerator, and go back to the bedroom alone, leaving him sitting there with that sad look on his face. I don't care anymore; I *can't* care anymore. If I keep caring, one way or another I'm afraid I'll wind up dead.

It's after dark when I get up and make it to the bathroom. When I'm done, I stumble down the hall to check my room and, when I see that the bed's been made with fresh sheets, I go in and lie down. I don't want to be in his bed. I don't want to be anywhere near him. All I want to do is manage to get through the next three days so the nightmare is over. As I lie there, I feel something on my face; I'm crying and I didn't even know it.

The next morning I wake to the sound of the shower in his bathroom. I go to my bathroom, splash some water on my face, and go straight into the living room. When he comes out of the bathroom, he gets the shock of his life.

I'm kneeling by the door. I have my pajamas on, but I'm kneeling there. Even though I'm not looking at his face, I can still see his expression in my peripheral vision: Pure disbelief. He walks over in front of me and just stands there, looking like he's trying to figure out what to say. And here's what comes out:

"What are you doing?"

Wow, brilliant. So much for thinking on the fly, hot shot. "What does it look like I'm doing?" I spit.

Bewilderment is written all over him and his voice is almost pleading. "Trish, you don't have to do this. Just . . ."

"Yes. I do. I made a commitment, and I intend to live up to it." I can feel my face getting red and my blood pressure going up. "And do you know why?"

He shakes his head, so I start in. "Because I'm an honorable person. Because when I make a promise, I intend to keep it. Because I don't give up easily. Because I'm kind, and considerate, and *helpful*," I say with emphasis, and now I'm getting angry because I can feel the tears, "and smart, and funny, and some people might even find me attractive and think that I can cook." Now I'm almost choking because I'm trying so hard not to cry. "So yes, I have to do this. You can hate me and abuse me and mistreat me and hurt me, but I live up to my promises. I'm almost done and, when I am, I'll go away and leave you alone and you won't ever have to see me again. But until then, know that if you wanted to kill me, you should've done a better job." I'm shaking and tears are rolling down my face, but I refuse to sob. If there's a shred of dignity left to hang onto, I'm looking for it and trying to clutch it in both hands.

In that moment, I see something on Clint's face, a sadness there, some kind of pain, something digging into him and wounding him and clawing at his insides. There's no way for me to know what it is, and he's certainly not going to tell me anything, but I see it. And even though I don't want to care, I do. I keep waiting, hoping he'll say something that will give me some insight, when he sits down opposite me in the chair and says, "Look at me. Please."

That's what I do. I look directly into his eyes, and I expect him to squirm, but he doesn't. He sighs and sits back like he's trying to start but he doesn't know how or where. "Dave talked to me. Trish, I . . ."

I turn my head away and hold up my palm to him. "You don't have to say anything. I don't want to know. Nothing you could say could change anything. It's not necessary." It's not that I'm angry or sad. I just don't want to be hurt anymore, and I get the feeling that whatever this is, it will hurt.

"Yes, I do. I have to say this." He takes a big, deep breath, then blows it out like he's a deflating balloon. "It needs to be said. Trish, I don't hate you. I know that's what you think, but I don't. Matter of fact, that's exactly the opposite of what I feel." Now I'm curious where he's going with this, because I know what it sounds like he means but I also know that just can't be. "It was wrong of me to bring you here and refuse to share anything of myself with you." I want to yell, *Damn right!*, but I don't, just wait. "You need to know that I was married. My wife left me. She'd been fucking my best friend for three years and I didn't know it. She left me *and* the girls, just walked away. When he dumped her six months later, she called and wanted to come home, but I said no. I couldn't trust her." He gets a weird look on his face, and then he says, "So she killed herself."

For the first time in my life, I truly don't know what to think or say. I mean, what can you say to that? "I've felt like the lowest of the low. I felt responsible for her death. Everyone has told me that she was an adult, that she made that choice, not me, but I live in 'what-if land' every day. I've kind of slogged through life ever since, just trying to stay in the driver's seat long enough to raise my girls." He leans forward with his elbows on his knees and drops his face into his hands, then looks up at me again.

"When you walked up to me at the bar that night, you seemed kind and friendly, maybe a little naïve, and I thought, 'Here's a woman I could get to know. She looks safe.' And it scared the shit out of me. I tried everything

I could to stay away from you, but Dave was determined to get us together. I know why he did it, and I appreciate his attempts, but I think it was misguided. I'm obviously not fit to be partnered with anyone. Ever again. For the rest of my life."

He stops and stares at the carpet, a kind of exhausted resignation settling over him. "Trish, I brought you here and threw everything I had at you to get you to turn tail and run. Then I could say you weren't trustworthy, you didn't keep your commitments, you weren't worthy of my time, of me. I damn near killed you trying to get you to go and you just wouldn't. And every time you hung in there, I felt more drawn to you, even though I didn't want to. But last night I finally realized that it's *me* who's not worthy. *I'm* the worthless piece of crap. It's not you. It's *me*. And you'll never know how sorry I am for what I've put you through. You trusted me and I betrayed your trust at every juncture." He stands. "So I'm going to go and get dressed. If you want to go, I'll be glad to take you home. I broke the promise, not you. You honored it. Matter of fact," he says, his voice almost too low for me to hear, "you're probably the most honorable person I've ever met in my life."

I watch him retreat down the hallway and disappear into his bedroom. My head is spinning and I don't know how to process the things he's just said. But I realize that I've loved him since the first time I laid eyes on him. And that means one thing.

I have to leave.

He drives me home and carries all of my stuff into the house. When he's finished, he turns to me and says, "I know you probably don't ever want to see me again, but if I can ever do anything to help you, all you have to do is let me know." I can tell he wants to hug me, but when he moves toward me, I stick out my hand for a handshake. If I let him hug me, I know I'll never want to let go, and I'll be opening myself up to more pain and misery than I can handle. He takes my hand in both of his, then strokes a finger down the side of my face and walks out the door.

I cry for two days. I don't sleep, don't eat, don't shower, don't go anywhere. My bed becomes the tomb of my heart, the place where I try to bury it and it won't stay buried. It just keeps crying out for him. On Friday evening, I realize I could try to anesthetize it, so I shower, get dressed in black street clothes, and drive to the club. When I walk into the community area, a pair of arms wraps around me from behind and Dave hugs me tight.

"How ya doin', baby?" he whispers in my ear.

I choke back a sob. "I'm okay."

"You don't look okay. You look shot. Want a drink?"

"Yeah. Just a beer. If I drink anything stronger, well . . ."

"Uh-huh, I know. If you'll recall, that's how I met you, drinking away a broken heart." Leave it to Dave to cut straight to the chase. I take my beer and turn my back to the bar, not wanting him to see my face or the pain I know is there. "I know you're wondering if I've seen him or talked to him," he adds.

"No, I'm not." *And I'm a big fat-ass liar, too.* I wait. Dave wants me to ask, I can tell.

He lets me get two-thirds of the way through my beer before he finally says, "Trish, I've never seen him so broken."

Something's been bothering me all along, and I finally identify it in that instant. "You talk like you've known him for a long, long time. How long *have* you known Clint? What's the story there?"

Dave shakes his head. "I've known him for twenty-eight years." I spin around and stare at him, and I'm sure my eyebrows are in my hairline. "I was his stepdad until his mom and I divorced. He wasn't my son, but I raised him from the time he was seven."

Oh. My. GOD. *That's* why he'd gone to such lengths to try to get us together. They're not casual friends; he loves Clint like a son. "Trish, let me ask you something: Did he tell you about Christi? His wife?" I nod. "Do you realize you're the first person he's *ever* shared that with outside the family? He's never told another living soul. His friends only know what they've heard from the rumor mill; he's never discussed it with anyone."

My heart starts to tremble in a weird way that it never has before. Maybe I'm having a heart attack. I shake my head. "Doesn't matter. I can't trust him; I'll never be able to trust him. He almost killed me trying to get me to go away when he could've just said, 'Scram. Get out of here.' But he didn't. He just tormented me, tortured me, tried to destroy me. I can't just ignore that."

And then he drops the bomb. They could hear it across town, I'm sure. "That night I had to leave? When he did the anal work with you? He told me it was all he could do to stop himself from wrapping his arms around you and telling you that he was in love with you. He'd known it from that first night when you asked if you could sit next to . . ."

"STOP!" I slam my beer bottle down on the bar and several people nearby turn to stare, but I don't care. "None of that matters! I went to him in love and trust, and he used me and hurt me and broke me. I damn near lost my life trying to please him. If he can't say those three words to me himself, I sure as hell don't need to hear them from you!"

I hop down off the stool and make a beeline for the door. Behind me I hear Dave call out, "Trish? Honey, please . . ." but I keep going straight out the door to my car and drive away.

And I damn near get myself killed because I'm crying so hard I can't really see to drive.

When the doorbell rings, I panic. But when I look through the peephole, I'm infuriated. "What the *hell* do you want?"

"Trish, let me in." Before I can say no, Ron pushes the door open. "Holy shit, what's wrong with you?"

"None of your goddamn business. Get the hell out," I say. The chair across the room is too far away, but I make it there and drop into it, lifeless.

"Damn, Trish, you look horrible. Are you sick?" He actually looks a little concerned. I try not to let that sway me. I know it'll pass.

"As I said before, none of your goddamn business." There's something in me that is really pissed by the fact that he's asking any questions at all. He lost that privilege when he walked out.

"Can I do anything for you?" He really *does* sound concerned. Good.

"No. I just need to be alone."

"Did that sex god of yours hurt you?" There's this pseudo-compassionate look on his face, and it really infuriates me.

"You need to do whatever you came to do and get out." I let my eyelids drop and point at the door.

It's quiet for a few seconds, and then he says, "Look, if he hurt you, I'll just go and . . ."

Bile rises up in my throat and I have trouble breathing when I say, "Nothing anyone else could do could hurt me more than you have. Leave. Me. Alone. Go." It's a lie, but it's designed to wound, and I think it'll do the trick.

The air in the room shifts as I feel him get up and hear him walk down the hall. There's the sound of shuffling and rustling around, and then he comes back through the room with a box of his stuff. "You know where to find me if you need me," he says, and I look up to find his hand on the doorknob.

I try to find something supremely hurtful to say, and I come out with, "If I really needed you, I'd pretty much be fucked, now wouldn't I?"

Without a word, he walks out the door. And in that moment I hope I never see him again as long as I live.

Chapter 11

I try to stay away from the club. I'm terrified that I'll run into him there, and I'm not sure what I'll do if that happens. Breaking down would be the worst, and that's exactly what I'm afraid I'll do. It's best to just stay away.

When Dave calls and tells me he still needs to do an exit interview with me, I tell him I'll come if he makes sure that Clint's interview appointment is nowhere near the time of mine, and that Clint won't know when I'll be there. He sounds like he wants to try to change my mind, but in the end he promises that he'll honor my wishes. I go in and refuse to answer most of the questions he asks.

As I leave, he reminds me that the collaring ceremony is two weeks away on Saturday night. I shake my head but he tells me, "I hope you'll consider coming. Maybe there's someone who'll collar you." My mouth won't make words to answer, so I just run out the door, get in my car, and leave.

The days drag by, and I stop being sad and start to get angry. The second stage of grief, right? If he's so sorry for how he treated me, why hasn't he even called to check on me? Knowing how hurt I was, he doesn't even bother to follow up? The confusion I feel threatens to take me down, and my self-worth is at an all-time low, even lower than after Ron pulled his stunt. It's past time for me to job hunt, but no one would hire me because of the shape I'm in now.

On the Thursday before the collaring ceremony, my doorbell rings. I'm afraid it's Clint, but when I open the door, there stands Dave. "Hi, sweetie. Can I come in and talk to you?"

I say nothing, just push the door open wider and motion for him to come in. I point to a chair and he takes a seat. "Would you like something to drink?" I ask and realize my voice sounds hollow and disconnected.

"No, no, that's okay. I just wanted to check on you. You doing okay?" He does look genuinely concerned.

"Yeah, I'm fine."

"You don't *sound* fine."

"I'm fine."

He waits for a bit, looking around and tapping his fingertips together. "You know he's hurting, don't you?" he finally says.

"*He's* hurting? Oh, wow, whatever shall we do?" I spit back. The pain that drifts like a cloud over Dave's face makes me instantly sorry. "That wasn't like me. I don't want him to hurt. But there's nothing I can do about it."

"Could you at least talk to him? Just for a few minutes? I know he'd like to hear from you."

And that's it. I can't take any more, and I jump up and start to pace. "He'd like to hear from *me*? You know, he hurt me, emotionally and physically, and then brought me here and walked away. I thought he'd call in a few days, check on me, see if I was okay after he left me to seize on that bed, but he didn't. He hasn't. He won't. I know what he told me happened to his wife, but that's no excuse for treating me like shit."

"Trish, he just . . ."

I stop and glare at him. "Oh, stop it! Stop making excuses for him. He's a grown man." Dave drops his eyes to the floor. "So he had a crisis, an unfortunate thing happened to him. So what? Happens to people all the time and they don't treat the people around them like shit. I'm sorry. This conversation is over. I don't want to hear any more about him and I don't want to talk about him. If you've got something else to say, we can talk, but I'm finished with this."

He stops, then looks up at me. "I wanted you to know that a few of the Doms at the club have asked about you. They wanted to know if you and Clint had worked out a permanent contract, and I told them no. I think one of them will probably offer to collar you if you show up Saturday night."

I knock a knee out and fold my arms across my chest. "Yeah? And who might these Doms be?"

"Well, Steffen for one."

"What about the sub he was paired with?"

"They didn't get along too well. I think she was too young, just not mature enough."

"Oh. I see. Who else?"

"One of our regulars, a guy named Gary." Yeah, Gary from the grocery – of course he'd want to collar me. "Said he'd met you and he'd love to have you in his home."

"Anybody else?"

"Yeah. Do you know Hank?" I shake my head. "Master Hank" sounds too much like Mr. Hankie the Christmas Poo from *Southpark* to me. I don't think I can do that. I'm sure he's a nice guy, but no. "He's been around for awhile. And a young guy named Trevor. Nice looking, maybe late twenties, early thirties. He's seen you in the club and wondered if you were collared. I think he's interested. The subs he's worked with have told me he's very good, especially for his age."

"Anybody else?" I can't think of anything else to say.

"Nope. Not that I can recall. Don't you think those are enough?" He smiles at me. I'm not smiling.

"I guess. If I come, I can't guarantee I'll accept from any of them." I can't believe that many men would want me. Me? Really? Come on.

"Well, I wish you'd consider it. A couple of them would be really good catches. Come tomorrow night and check them out before Saturday. They'll be there, I'm sure, scoping out the uncollared subs."

I shrug. "Maybe I will."

"Fair enough." He stands and takes my hands, then puts his arms around me and holds me. "Remember when you asked me if we all held the subs afterward?"

There are tears in his eyes, and I nod, feeling mine start to burn. "Well, that's kind of what I'm doing right now."

I can't help it. I start to sob. I'm so tired and weak and brokenhearted that I just can't hold it in. "My adventure didn't turn out so good, I guess."

He rubs my back and it feels good, so good that I'd like to ask him to keep it up. "I think the adventure was fine. But it's like they say: It's not the fall that gets you – it's the sudden stop at the bottom."

That's certainly true.

On Friday night, I put some decent-looking fetwear in my bag and climb into my car. When I get to the club it's really, really busy. First thing I do is look around; no Clint. Good. I head to the locker room and change, then walk out into the big room and go to the bar.

"Hi, honey!" Dave sings out and comes around the bar to hug me. "I'm so glad you're here! Have a cosmo." He never forgets. Before I can even take a sip, someone says, "Trish?"

I turn to find Steffen standing beside me. "Hi, sir. How are you?"

"I'm good." He takes a long look at me. "You, however, don't look so good."

"Gee, thanks. Just what a girl wants to hear, sir." I take a big swig of my drink.

"I didn't mean it that way. So will you be here tomorrow night?"

Another swig and I reach out to Dave with my empty glass for another round of high-proof amnesia. "I'm thinking about it."

"Good. I think you'll be happy if you are." He grins at me.

I glare back at him. "And why would you think that, sir?"

He's a bit taken aback by my expression, I can tell. "Oh, no reason. Just want to see you show up, that's all." I take another swallow and he looks at me again. "I think I'm going to go mingle. It's good to see you though. Take care of yourself." With that, he gives me a peck on the cheek and walks away.

Dave hears me chuckle under my breath. "You're quite the dragon, aren't you, little one?" he asks.

"Yeah, that's me. Fire-breathing and man-eating. I'm a bad, bad girl."

"Listen to you. There's something I think you should know." He walks up closer so I can hear him better.

"Yeah? What's that?"

"He hasn't been here since he took you home. I don't think he's coming back." I think he wants me to say something, but I don't know what. "I've told him I think he needs to come on back, keep himself out and around people, but he's just holed up in that house. The girls are still at his mother's." He stops for a minute, tries to read my face, and then adds, "Trish, I'm worried about him."

"Yeah, but nobody was worried about me, especially the one person who should've been. I guess now you're going to tell me that he's in love with me."

"Yes, he is. He's admitted it to me. More than once. Trish, that's rare. We only get so many chances at happiness."

That's when I start laughing. I know part of it is the liquor, but it just strikes me so damn funny. "Happiness? Seriously? You know, Dave, what I saw when I was there was a man who wasn't happy. He was a man who wanted the woman in his home gone. Guess that's just a pattern with him, huh?"

The minute the words are out of my mouth, I regret them. A pained expression flashes across Dave's face. When he speaks, he cuts right into me. "Gee, Trish, I never had you pegged as someone who could be so cruel. I guess I didn't know you at all." He throws down the cloth he's been wiping the bar with and stalks off, leaving the two younger guys to manage the drinking crowd.

Shit. Now I've hurt Dave. I didn't mean to do that. I head out the side door to find him and apologize and, when I do, I hear a phone ring around the corner of the building. I stop to listen before I round it.

"Hello? Oh, hi. Yeah, I'm outside. I really don't want to . . . yeah, she's here. I did, but she's made up her mind. Look, if you want to have a relationship with somebody, you're going to have to be open with them." Then I hear him say, "Can I ask you something? I know what you said, but what was so important about her staying out of the office? So important that you'd do something like that to her when all she did was try to help you?" There's silence, and I wish I could hear the answer to that one because Dave responds with, "Well, that's the damn dumbest thing I've ever heard. That's what it was? For god's sake, Clint, this was supposed to be a relationship, not a goddamn emotional obstacle course! The woman is wounded down deep, maybe too deep. She doesn't trust anybody now, not even me, and I don't blame her. You need to know that I rigged the drawing. I wanted the two of you to be . . . Oh, shit. Does she know too? Damn. No wonder she doesn't trust me either. I don't have any right to call you stupid. I'm pretty damn stupid myself. Now I know why she kept saying that I was wrong to throw the two of you together." He stops, then says, "I don't know. I'm trying to get her to come, but I doubt she will. Her heart's frosted up pretty good. She said some things a little while ago that were so mean I couldn't believe they were coming from her. I think there's been too much damage done, son. You need to just get over her and go on, but I think you need to wait a while longer, maybe get some professional help. You're not ready." There's a long silence. "Yeah, son, I'm sorry too. Let me know if there's anything I can do for you. I love you, you know that. Yeah. Okay, talk to you soon." I hear him let out a deep sigh and I hightail it for the door before he can know that I'm there.

I go straight to the locker room, change into my street clothes, and walk back out. Dave's not back at the bar, so I don't have to say anything to him as I leave. I just get in my car and drive away.

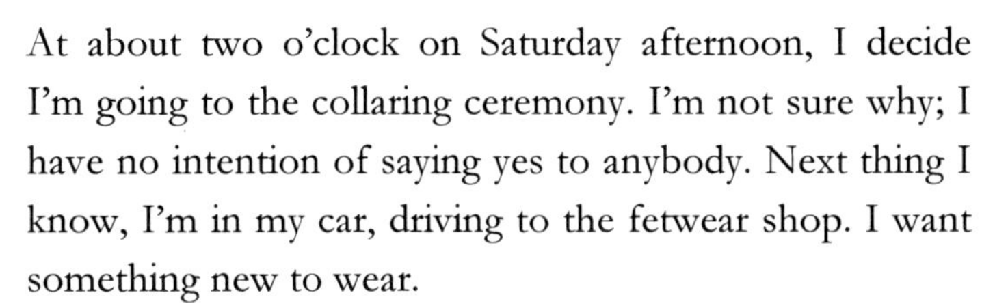

At about two o'clock on Saturday afternoon, I decide I'm going to the collaring ceremony. I'm not sure why; I have no intention of saying yes to anybody. Next thing I know, I'm in my car, driving to the fetwear shop. I want something new to wear.

The girl who'd waited on me before is there. She seems glad to see me, and she helps me go through the racks. I find a pretty peacock-blue dress that's cut very low in the back, ass cleavage low, and has cutouts in the front. The color is beautiful, and they even have some platform stilettos to match, so I get them too. I'm looking for jewelry to go with it when I notice that the expensive collar is gone. "Hey, did someone buy that collar?" I ask her.

She smiles. "Yeah, they sure did! I couldn't believe it. Some lucky sub is going to be very, very happy." *Not me*, I want to scream.

I pay for my outfit and head back home. By six, I'm ready to roll. The collaring ceremony is at seven, so I climb into my car and head downtown. I still have no idea why I'm going.

I'm guessing I'll find out when I get there.

Chapter 12

I've never seen the place so crowded. I sit at the bar, drinking a cosmo served to me by a cute young guy. Dave is nowhere in sight.

Before I can get half of it down, I hear a voice beside me. "Well, well, well – don't you look beautiful!" It's Steffen, and he's all smiles.

"Hi, sir."

"Hi yourself." He looks me up and down. "That's quite a body you've got under that dress. Oh, wait – I've seen it before, haven't I?" he whispers as he leans into my ear. "I wouldn't mind seeing it again. And again. And again and again."

"Uh-huh. Okay." That's all I say, my voice flat and face blank.

Apparently I've stunned him so badly that he can't speak. He finally croaks out, "Okay, well, I'll talk to you later." When I turn, he's gone. Did I scare him off? I have no idea.

There's still a problem with getting my drink down because next in line is Gary. He sidles up to me at the bar and says, "Well, hello there! Remember me?"

"Yes, I do, sir," I say, looking down into my drink. "As I recall, you work in a grocery store."

"I *manage* a grocery store." He looks quite proud of himself. Nothing like produce to give a guy the big head.

"That's right. I remember now."

"I remember you *well*," he assures me. "So rumor has it you're here for the collaring ceremony."

Wow, genius, how did you ever guess? "Well, I'm here. And I think there's a collaring ceremony going on tonight. So yeah, I guess I'll be here while the collaring ceremony is going on, sir."

"Good! I hope I see you later tonight," he says. Before he walks away, he takes my hand and kisses it. I think that was supposed to score him some points. It does not.

A couple more guys are watching me from a distance. One of them is a gorgeous young guy, maybe twenty-four to twenty-eight, not quite thirty. Ah, Trevor, I'm betting. The guy Dave told me about. That's all I need, a man to raise. He is cute, though, but I don't think I could be a sub to a guy young enough to be my son.

I just sit there, sucking on my drink, when I feel a presence beside me, and I know who it is before I even look up. "Good evening, Dave," I say into the glass.

"Hey, honey. I didn't think you'd be here."

Before I can stop myself, I snort, "I didn't think I'd be here either." I hesitate for a second, then say, "Hey, about the other night, I . . ."

He shakes his head. "Don't worry about it. Really. It's okay. And by the way, I know you know about the pairing. I'm sorry, really I am. I had no right to do that." There's a long pause, and then he says, "Trish, you don't owe me anything, and the same goes for Clint. But please, honey, if he shows up tonight, could you at least be kind to him? Sorry, but I'm begging here. If not for him or me, do it for yourself so you have no regrets later on, okay?"

"Don't worry about it. I won't have to be kind. I'll just leave." My cosmo is gone, so I hand the glass to the bartender to refill. "I don't think either of us should have to be that uncomfortable, and he was here first, so I'll gladly step aside."

Dave's sadness wraps around me, and I wish I could turn back time. I wish I'd never opened that door, wish I'd just let Clint lose that account, wish I hadn't cared so much, but I can't take any of it back. "Trish, honey, just do what you think you have to do." I turn to tell him I don't feel like I have a choice, but he's gone.

In a little while they begin the ceremony. One by one, subs go up and stand on the stage. Each one waits and eventually a Dominant comes forward and asks her to accept his or her collar. Some of them are obviously very much in love, and some look like this is their last hope and they've been backed into a corner. Vance comes up when his name is called. An older, very attractive Domme starts toward the stage, but out of nowhere, the big Domme comes rushing up, pushes her away, and runs onto the stage to claim him. He looks like he's going to burst with joy. I guess it's true – there really *is* someone for everyone.

We all get a surprise about halfway through. The mean-looking Dom who got the pretty young girl in the pairing? He offers her the pricey collar from the fetwear shop and, to my relief, she looks thrilled. When he puts it on her, his features soften, and I see the man she probably saw during her two weeks with him. They look very happy, and I'm glad for them both.

There's a hand on my shoulder, and I turn. The guy standing there is someone I've never seen before. "Hi. Can I help you with something?" I ask him quietly so as not to interrupt the ceremony.

"Yeah, uh, yes ma'am. A guy asked me to give this to you." He hands me a box and, before I can thank him, he's gone.

It's a flat box, about twelve inches square and less than two inches tall, with a wooden hasp and a hinge. I look around but I don't see anyone I know. There's a card on top of the box, so I pick it up with shaking hands and open it. The spotlights above the bar are my only source of light, so I move into one pool of brightness to read it. As the words come off the page and into my mind, my heart breaks all over again.

Dear Trish,

Words can't begin to describe the way I feel. I'm so sorry and so broken that I don't know how I'm going to get through tomorrow. I already had enough regret for one man, and now I have enough for two. I know you can't forgive me, and I don't expect you to. Just know that what happened wasn't what was in my heart. It was just a man trying desperately to not love a woman and failing miserably.

The item in this box doesn't belong to me. It belongs to you. It has since the day I first saw it. I won't tell you when that day was because you wouldn't believe me anyway. But know that every day for the rest of my life I'll think of it and what it would've looked like on you. And I'll remember how badly I messed up and hurt you. If there's anything I learned in my time with you, it's that I don't deserve a woman like you, and I'll never try to find another.

I also think I should tell you that Mr. Norsworthy called. He went on and on about how appreciative he was for your help that day. Then he offered me a contract, not just for his own office but for all of their offices. It'll wind up being about $600,000. That's not a fortune, but it will help me start the girls' college fund, something I've wanted to do for awhile but couldn't afford. So the thing that I punished you for will allow my girls to go to college. And I don't even know what to think about that except to be sorrier than before, if that's even possible.

Anyway, that's all I wanted to say, except that I love you and I've loved you since the first time I saw you. I know I didn't act like it, but it's true. When you think of me, please try to remember something good, something fun, something sweet that we did together and not just the bad things. Don't worry, though. The bad things won't be forgotten. I'll remember them forever. They're seared into my memory like a nightmare I can't wake from.

Find someone who'll love you for the beautiful, precious woman you are, someone who can do a better job of it than I could. I'll love you always, my Vännan.

Forever,
Clint

My hands are trembling so wildly that I can't get the box open. I look at a guy sitting next to me at the bar and ask, "Would you help me, please? I can't get this open."

"Sure, honey. Here," he says as he takes it from me. He opens it and, before I can even get a glimpse inside, he murmurs out, "Whoaaaaaa. That's really something." I reach for it and turn the open box to see.

It's a collar. It's not just any collar. I thought the one I'd seen at the fetwear shop, the one the Dom gave his new sub, was the most beautiful collar in the world.

I was wrong.

There's a narrow band of yellow gold top and bottom, and the wide band in the middle is white gold, I presume, maybe even platinum. Around each side, the white is cut out to show the yellow gold backing it. It looks to be laser cut, very lace-like, delicate, and intricate. I take a closer look and I can see hummingbirds, butterflies, and dragonflies. There's a turtle, a frog, and a tiny mouse looking out of the lacework. Right in the center front, there's a solid, uncut expanse of white gold about three inches wide, and there's something engraved in it. In the light of the bar, in the very seat I was sitting in when I saw Clint for the first time, I see one word engraved on the collar.

Vännan.

My heart sinks into my stomach and everything is blurry through my tears. I stare at the collar, so delicate and fine, and I remember the nights we lay together in his big bed, rocking into each other, our hearts beating in synchronicity. I remember the day he kissed me and I knew something was happening between us. And suddenly, I try to remember that last day and I can't. It's gone. All I can remember is the first time he smiled for me, and I begin to sob. I don't know what to do – I'm crying so hard that I can't get up and walk out, but I can't just sit there. And then the worst possible thing happens.

They call my name.

Before I can stop myself, my feet are on the move. The people in the room are like water, rolling away and creating a path to the stage for me, the Red Sea parting and dry land appearing, sending me on to the Promised Land, my own fair hell. I wish they'd been a little less helpful, but they aren't, damn them. I get to the stage, manage to climb the two steps, and stand there, my face a mess, my mascara running, I'm sure. Then the voice calls out, "This sub awaits collaring. Is there a Dom who will claim her for his own?"

I see movement in the crowd. To my horror, Steffen and Gary both show up at the edge of the stage, and Trevor is hovering nearby. It doesn't matter that Clint isn't here; I can't give my heart to any of these men. It isn't mine to give away anymore.

Steffen and Gary mount the steps and I'm almost in a panic. That's when I look down and see what I'm holding in my hand.

The collar. I didn't realize I was still clutching it until that moment, and when both of them make it up onto the stage, I do what I have to do, what I need to do, what I want to do more than anything in that moment. I pull it open and slip it on my neck. They both stare at me like I'm insane, but it feels right. And there's only one thing left to do. I drop to my knees and fall prostrate on the floor. I know I'll still be here tomorrow morning, but I don't care. I want everyone to just go away and let me have this moment, this snapshot in time when I give myself to a man without his desire or knowledge and take the pain it offers me.

The room gets quiet. There are no voices and no movement. I don't know how long I'm here, but it seems like forever before I feel a hand on my arm and I know who it is without looking up. Dave whispers down to me, "Trish? Honey? Let's get up. You can't stay here. Come on, I'll help you."

"No! Leave me alone! I want to stay here until he gets here, Dave, please?" It's too late to save face. I'm embarrassing myself and I don't care.

"He's not coming. Honey, come on. We can go to my office. It'll be okay." He takes my arm and tries to help me up, but I fight him off, push at him, lash out.

From the back of the room I hear a voice growl, "Get your hands off my sub." There's a ripple of whispers across the crowd, and I wonder what's going on, but I don't care. This is where I want to stay.

Dave's voice is different when I hear him reply, "I'm sorry, sir," and his footsteps echo as he climbs down off the stage. I hear another set of footsteps approach me, and a presence comes into my space. There's energy and heat radiating from it and I wait, not daring to hope, until a palm rests on my head and there's a whisper in my ear.

"My Vännan, come to your love. Please, baby?"

I can't see him through my tears, but I know his arms, and in a split second I'm in them and gripping his neck like there's no tomorrow. I hear that deep, warm voice say, "I'm so sorry, angel. I didn't think you wanted to see me, but I couldn't stay away. Please, please, don't give up on me."

He's squeezing me so tightly that I have trouble pulling away from him but when I do, I don't say a word. I just point to my neck. His hands wipe away my tears, but they do nothing for his own, his face slick with them, his cheeks shiny and soaked, and I just stare at him, at those beautiful eyes. The only thing I can rasp out in reply is, "Oh god, please don't hurt me anymore."

He pulls me into his chest and leans into my ear, his breath warm on my skin when he whispers back, "Never again. Never, ever again." As he leans back from me, he takes a look at my tear-stained face and the gift of his love around my neck, and he presses his lips to mine.

And there they are, soft and warm and sweet, those lips I tasted over and over, that I hoped would eventually say something magical and wonderful to me. I feel his arms wrap tight around me and my fingers wind into his hair, holding his face to me, begging without words, pleading for something, anything, to hang onto. He hands it to me on a silver platter when he murmurs into my ear, sultry and low, "Trish, I love you. I want to be the Dom, the man, you trust and look up to, who never lets you down and always walks beside you, who never lets you fall or drift away. You gave me your love, and I didn't see it for the rare, precious thing it is. But, baby, it's really all I need to make my life complete."

He watches as I take the collar off and hand it to him. At first I can see that he's horrified, and then he understands what I'm doing, what I'm asking of him. I stand and wait. Coming up off of his knees, he faces me with the collar in his hands. He takes a deep, ragged breath and asks, in front of the entire room, "Submissive, I come today to ask for your service and to offer you this token of my devotion as your Dominant for all my days. What say you to my offering?"

I smile and start to cry again. He reaches over and wipes my eyes with the back of his hand, and I try again. "Sir, I desire to call you Master and to serve under your care and devotion as your dedicated submissive for all my days."

"Then kneel before me and accept my collar." I kneel in a perfect presentation pose and Clint leans down to slip the collar around my neck, then takes a tiny padlock from his pocket and snaps it shut on the hasps at the back of the collar. I can't help it – I reach up and finger its delicacy, the warmth of his hands still in the metal. As soon as I hear the lock snap, I lean forward and kiss his shoes, first the left, then the right. When I rise upright again, he reaches a hand down to me and says, "Submissive, come to your master."

I'm in his arms. That's the only place I've wanted to be. As he hugs me tight, I peek over his shoulder and see Dave, tears rolling down his face. Our eyes meet, and he gives me a thumbs-up as he disappears in the direction of his office.

When Clint takes my hand, he leads me off the stage and down the back hallway amid gasps, murmurs, and whispers, and I wonder where we're going. He opens the door to the nicest of the private rooms and closes it behind us once we're inside. "What are we doing here?"

He smiles. "We're consummating our union. At least I hope we are." He puts a hand on each of my cheeks, holds my face to his, and looks into my eyes. "I don't want to fuck you. I want to make love to you. What do you say to that?"

"I say turn loose of me so I can get my clothes off!" I laugh through my tears.

He grins. "You don't have to tell me twice!"

"It's really quiet out there. Where'd everybody go?"

My cheek resting on his chest, I hear the rumble of a chuckle come up from down deep inside him. "I'm betting they've all gone home. It's," he says, looking at his watch, "almost three thirty in the morning."

"Oh god! How will we get out of here?" I gasp.

He laughs and kisses the tip of my nose. "Shit, I've got a key, girl. I can get out of here anytime. I just don't want to right now." He pulls me close again and kisses me, then kisses down my chest and takes a nipple in his mouth. "God, I missed you, little sub," he mumbles around it.

"I missed you too, Master," I groan as his hand slips between my legs, and pretty soon his tongue replaces it.

He laughs again. "I can tell!" I'm so wet I'm dripping. Or maybe that's his offering to me. He's only filled me up about nine times since we came in here.

"You're insatiable! But I'm not complaining." His hair is soft as I run my fingers through it. "Clint, do you have some kind of plan? Where do we go from here? How does this work."

There's a solid, peaceful look on his face when my eyes meet his from down between my thighs. "If you mean long-term, then I want a permanent relationship. If you mean short-term, you've got two little girls to meet tomorrow if you think you're ready."

My eyes close, and I sigh and smile. “I’m ready if you are.”

He grins. “Readier than I’ve ever been.” And then he makes me squeal.

Chapter 13

"Mrs. Winstead?"

I turn to see a teacher running toward me. It's Mrs. Cox, Hailee's teacher. "Yes! Hi! How are you?"

She gives me a warm smile. "I'm great! Good to see you. I saw you passing by my door and I wanted to catch you. I have something for you." She hands me an envelope.

"What's this?" I'm hoping it's not bad news.

"I think you'll like it. It's just a copy – I have to keep the original for their portfolio. Don't let Hailee know I've given you this, please? And please don't open it until you get it home, maybe share it with Mr. Winstead."

I can't imagine what it could be. "Um, thanks. I'll do that. Is Hailee doing okay in class?"

"Oh, yes ma'am. She's doing very well. She's a very happy little girl, and now I understand why." She's smiling at me kind of strangely, and I really can't figure out what's going on.

"That's good. Please let us know if there's anything we need to be doing with her."

She shakes her head. "She's a very smart little girl too, Mrs. Winstead. Just keep doing what you're doing."

"Please, it's Trish," I tell her with a smile of my own.

"Trish. I'm Wendy. And she is smart, and very polite too. More so than her classmates."

I really smile then. "Her dad expects that of them. They're being raised to be respectful and considerate of others."

She makes a face. "I wish I could say that about the rest of my class!" She laughs, and I have to chuckle. I've seen some of McKenna and Hailee's classmates – she's not exaggerating. "Well, it was good talking to you. Take care." She walks away, then turns and says, "And congratulations. Enjoy that." She points at the envelope and then walks on down the hallway.

"Here I am!" a little voice calls out. Hailee's been at academic team practice. They start them early these days, and I hear she's doing very well. They won't let anyone in to observe yet; they say it just makes the kids too nervous. I've been on a stage, naked, in front of dozens of people. I can certainly relate.

"Come on, honey. We're having guests for dinner tonight and I've got to get home. And we've got to stop and pick McKenna up at Taylor's house." As she takes my hand and we head to the car, I look down at one of the two little girls who've made me the luckiest woman in the world. Being the woman in their lives has been one of the sweetest adventures I could've ever been handed, and I'm thankful for it every second of every day. They don't know it yet, but their biggest Christmas gift from Clint and me will be the one I've spent the morning arranging – my adoption of both of them. Once it's finalized, I'll have the children I never dreamed I'd have.

After we pick up McKenna from her friend's house, I spend the drive home telling them about the next day and how their Grandma Marta and Nanny Angela, Clint's mother and her partner, are coming to take them to see Santa at the mall. Marta invited Angela into the bed she shared with Dave, which was okay with him, but he said it didn't take long before he realized that Angela wanted to top them both, and Dave couldn't be her bottom. So he and Marta divorced amicably, and they're all still friends; actually, sometimes the three of them still play together. The girls call him Grandpa, and they always will. Clint calls him Dad, and that's a wonderful thing. Marta, Angela, and I have been going shopping together, having lunch, things like that. I love them both. And is it a little weird that I've had sex with my father-in-law and everyone in the family knows it? Yeah, but it appears that I'm the only one who finds it weird. Nobody else seems to mind. It's a strange and wonderful little family.

"Look what I brought!" Sheila calls out as soon as she gets in the front door that evening. "I know how Clint loves my scalloped potatoes!"

"Yes, he does. You're putting me to shame, you know that?" I laugh. "Why don't you just make them for your own man and leave mine alone?"

"She does, babe. Maybe a little too much," Steffen laughs and kisses the side of Sheila's neck.

"Oh, Sir, do it again," she whispers and he gives her a nip.

"You two leave the play until you get home. Kids, remember?" I point down the hallway.

"I know. What a shame too. I'm past ready," Steffen growls into Sheila's ear and I hear her breath hitch. They've been a couple for three months now. The first night I dragged Sheila with Clint and me to the club, Steffen latched onto her and wouldn't let go. It took him six weeks to convince her to scene with him, but once she did, she never looked back. I never thought Sheila would fall into the lifestyle, but she's in hook, line, and sinker.

Dinner is lovely. I've made my famous pork roast, Sheila's scalloped potatoes earn her a kiss on the cheek from Clint, and the Brussels sprouts that the girls insisted on have the buttery flavor that they love. Everyone's had a big piece of my applesauce cake for dessert, and Steffen and Sheila have said their goodbyes with promises to the girls that they'll come and take them on a safari to the new wild animal park.

Hailee and McKenna are in their beds, and when I check on them, they're both sawing logs. I retreat to the bedroom where there's a sexy, gorgeous man waiting for me, already in the bed and keeping it warm. "They're out," I tell him with a grin. "I think it's time to play, Master, if it pleases you."

"Oh, it will definitely please me," he groans as he pulls me down with him, then strips off my short gown and panties and folds me into him. He looks down at me with those sparkling eyes and says, "It would please me greatly to fuck you and satisfy you. Are you ready for me, sub?"

"Yes, Master. I ache for you," I whisper to him. Then I shoot upright and almost yell, "Oh! Wait! I forgot something!" He looks at me like I'm nuts. "Permission to get out of the bed, Master?"

"What's this about?"

"Something Wendy, um, Mrs. Cox, Hailee's teacher, gave me today at the school. I forgot all about it. May I go and get it, Master? She said we would enjoy it."

He shrugs. "Of course. Permission granted. Then get your ass right back here. I want to pound it."

I shiver all over at his words and my nipples harden until they're painful. "Yes, Master. I'll be right back." I jet naked into the living room and find my purse. The envelope is a little crinkled but otherwise fine. I run back down the hall and almost slide past the bedroom door, then close it behind me and jump on the bed, envelope in hand.

He reaches for it and looks at it. "What is this?"

"I have no idea. She just told me to wait until I was home with you before I opened it." My hands are shaking. "Open it! I'm so excited! Wonder what it is?"

He opens the envelope, pulls out a sheet of paper, and instantly his eyes get misty. That scares me. "What is it? What's wrong? What does it say?"

He shakes his head and smiles. "Listen." Then he sits up, crosses his legs yoga-fashion, and starts to read.

"'What I want for Christmas by Hailee Winstead.' Honey, I . . ." He swallows hard. "I don't know if I can get through this."

"Try, okay?" He's making me really nervous.

"Okay, here goes." He takes a deep breath. "'My name is Hailee Winstead. I am eleven years old. When school got out in the spring, I was very sad because I would miss my friends. I have a nice dad, but no mom. My mom left us and then she died. I spent most of the summer with my grandmas. We went to the zoo and on picnics. When I came home from their house, my dad took us to dinner at a fancy restaurant that didn't have burgers. A lady came to dinner with us too, and she was very nice. I liked her a lot. My dad said they were dating.' Hmmm . . . so that's what it's called!" Clint laughs. I have to giggle.

"'She came to our house a lot and took us places, and helped us pick out clothes. She cooks very good food. Just a little bit after school started, my dad told me and my sister that he and the nice lady were getting married. I asked if I could be in the wedding and she said of course, we both could. And my sister and me got very pretty dresses to wear. So on Labor Day they got married. It was really pretty. We went to a huge lake and stood way up in the air on a bluff by a big rock. The woods workers made us a new road.'" We know she meant the forestry workers who cleared the fire road so we could drive back to the lake. She doesn't know anything about that rock – thank goodness. "'She didn't wear a big puffy white dress, just a nice little blue one. Her name is Trish. She's older than my daddy, but she's pretty even if she is old.'" Clint snickers and I slap his leg.

"'Now when I come home she's there to help me with my school work. She cooks us dinner and we help. We all clean up after dinner. She does our laundry and helps me with academic team stuff. And she drives us around. She dances in the living room with my dad and he smiles all the time now.'" I hear a hitch in Clint's voice. "'She does all the mom things, so my sister and me asked her can we call you mom and she cried and said yes.'" Tears are rolling down my face and Clint is sniffing. "I don't know if I can get through this part. 'So when I had to write what I want for Christmas . . .'" he takes a big shuddering breath. "'. . . I want Santa to take my toys and give them to boys and girls who don't have any because I already got what I wanted to ask him for. I got a mom. The end.'"

His eyes find my weepy ones, and two big, fat, crystal teardrops meander down his cheeks. "Trish, I . . ."

I put my finger to his lips. "Shhhh. Don't say anything. Whatever you were going to say, I already know. You've said it all dozens of times already, every day and every night, but I'm the lucky one, hear me? I'm the lucky one. I just have one question: Are you happy?"

He wipes his eyes with his hand, and then they fix on mine, melting my insides and warming my heart. "I'm so happy that sometimes I think my heart will just explode.

And you know what?" I shake my head. "Christmas is three weeks away, and Santa can keep *my* toys. I've already gotten the only thing I didn't have that I really wanted." He leans in and kisses me. "Merry Christmas, my wife. I love you more than you'll ever know."

"I love you too, my husband. Always and forever." In seconds he's inside me, stroking in me, filling me with love and heat and passion.

Oh, hell yeah – Santa can keep my toys too.

ABOUT THE AUTHOR

Deanndra Hall lives in far western Kentucky with her partner of 30+ years and three crazy little dogs. She spent years writing advertising copy, marketing materials, educational texts, and business correspondence, and designing business forms and doing graphics design. After reading a very popular erotic romance book, her partner said, "You can write better than this!" She decided to try her hand at a novel. In the process, she fell in love with her funny, smart, loving, sexy characters and the things they got into, and the novel became the Love Under Construction series.

Deanndra enjoys all kinds of music, kayaking, working out at the local gym, reading, and spending time with friends and family, as well as working in the fiber and textile arts. And chocolate's always high on her list of favorite things!

On the Web and my blog: www.deanndrahall.com

Email: DeanndraHall@gmail.com

Facebook: facebook.com/deanndra.hall

Twitter: twitter.com/DeanndraHall

Substance B: substance-b.com/DeanndraHall

Mailing address: P.O. Box 3722, Paducah, KY 42002-3722

Here's a sneak peek from some of the author's other titles . . .

From Laying a Foundation, Book 1 in the **Love Under Construction Series**

"I think everything is as ready as we can get it," Nikki told Tony as she stood in the kitchen on that evening, looking around.

"Then I guess I'll lock up and we'll call it a day," He shuffled off to lock the front door. Nikki turned to lock the back door, then turned off the kitchen lights. As she passed the island in the middle of the kitchen, a pair of strong hands grabbed her around the waist and lifted her onto the island.

"Yeesh! You scared the bejesus out . . ." she tried to say, but Tony covered her mouth with his and kissed her – hard. When he pulled back, she was breathless. "Wow, that was . . ." and he gave her a repeat performance, this time running both hands up under her top and peeling it off, then unbuttoning and unzipping her shorts. "You're . . ."

"Determined to have you. Right now. Want it? Say yes, baby," he murmured into her neck, then kissed her again, sucking her lower lip in between his.

"Yesssssss," she moaned, and he dug his fingers into her waist and picked her up. She promptly wrapped her legs around him, her arms clasped around his neck. They made it as far as the dining room table, biting each other's lips, tongues lashing into each other, before he sat her down on it, yanked her shorts off, then peeled off his tee and jeans. He climbed up onto the table with her and stared down at her in the darkness, his eyes intense, almost glowing.

"I should take you right here," he hissed into her ear, then bit her neck. Instead of making it easy for him, Nikki managed to wriggle away from him and took off running, giggling the whole time.

She made it as far as the foyer. Tony caught up with her, grabbed her around the waist, and spun her to look at him. "You're not getting away this time, little girl," he snarled at her. "I've got you and I'm not letting you go." This time, he reached around her and snapped the hooks of her bra loose, then locked his fingers into his boxer briefs, slid them down, and stepped out of them. Nikki purred when she got a glimpse of his cock, hard and waiting. He snatched her lacy hipsters off, then lifted her up again, and she wrapped her long, sculpted legs around his waist.

She wanted to kiss him again, long and slow, but before she could say or do anything, Tony wrapped his hands under her ass, lifted her a little higher, and impaled her on his rigid cock. Nikki stifled a scream as he bored into her pussy and showed no mercy, and Tony groaned and wedged her between his body and the wall, pistoning into her like a four-stroke engine as he held her there. He bit her neck again and, in turn, she bit his shoulder just like she'd done in the back of the SUV earlier in the day. He moaned into her ear, "I just wanna fuck you until I can't fuck you anymore. You are so goddamn sexy that you make me crazy for you."

"Then fuck me," she whispered back. "Fuck me hard. Just pound me until I scream for you to stop."

"Like I'd listen," he snickered and tied into her. His mouth found hers, and he kissed her so hard that she was sure he'd bruised her lips, then he latched onto her neck again and kissed, sucked, and bit it until she was nearly mad. He worked fast and hard, enjoying her cries against his collarbone, the pulses of her hot, wet sheath around his cock, and the hardness of her rigid peaks against his chest. He wished he could stop time or at least pause it, make a mental picture of them together, freeze the intensity of the sparks she gave off as her flint and his stone came together, as one's body burnished the other's to brilliance in that moment, so he could always recall it. Wanting to capture it all so he could enjoy it again later, sit in his office and think about it, picture her in his mind while he was at a jobsite, dream about her as she lay beside him sleeping in the night, he listened to her, soaked in the feel of her skin. He waited as long as he could before he poured himself into her in a gasping, moaning thrust that tuned her up until he was sure that Helene could hear them, even down at her house. Hell yeah, he hoped she could.

His possession of her body was too much for Nikki, and she tightened and came around him, screaming out, her fingers in his hair. When he stopped, she leaned in and locked her lips onto his, holding his face against hers until she couldn't breathe. "Sweet mother of god, babe, what's gotten into you today?" she panted when she finally broke the kiss.

"You. You're under my skin. Permanently. And I'm not complaining – not at all!" he laughed, then kissed her again. "I think it's about time I started living a more spontaneous life, stop planning everything out to the letter, start fucking you when I want, where I want, how I want, and making you want it too. And do you want it?" he asked with a seriousness that startled her.

"Want it? God, I crave it. Just cut loose!" she laughed back and kissed him.

"Let's go finish this in the bedroom," he told her as he carried her up the stairs. "I'll show you 'cut loose!'"

Thirty minutes later, she was still overwhelmed with his pressure inside her, his big, dark hands on her pale skin like molten lava, molded to her, pouring over her, twisting and pulling her nipples, flicking and stroking her clit. The sight of him above her drove her to the edge until his eyes closed and she saw that look on his face that said he was lost in ecstasy, lost in her. That look was all she needed; her own need consumed her and, as he buried himself in her over and over, she rasped her clit against his pelvis and came, repeating his name like a prayer. Within seconds, he groaned out his own climax. The liquid fire of his seed filled her, and she fell onto his chest, panting and moaning. His arms encircled her and tightened against her skin, and she'd never felt so desirable or so loved, so satisfied and so hungry for more.

"Are you trying to kill me?" she asked as he burrowed his face into her hair and kissed the top of her head.

"Yes. Death by sex," he chuckled as she licked his nipple.

"Correction: Death by great sex. Big difference," she giggled as he kissed the top of her head again. "But what a way to go!"

From Tearing Down Walls,
Book 2 in the
Love Under Construction Series

The club was starting to fill up, and the bar was busier than usual. Laura was drawing a couple of beers from a tap when she heard a woman at the bar say, "Holy shit, who's that? That's one extremely tall, dark, and hot Dom. Wonder if he's got a sub?" Laura turned to see who she was talking about and nearly fainted.

It was Vic Cabrizzi. And it was a Vic Cabrizzi she'd never seen before.

The mild-mannered man who'd sidled up to the bar and tried to make small talk with her was nowhere in this guy. Vic was six feet and eight inches of pure, dark, steaming sex in leather. He had the top half of his elbow-length black hair pulled up in a half-tail with a leather wrap, and his torso looked like it was trying to escape through the skin-tight black tee he was wearing. As he made his way toward the bar, the crowd parted to let him through as though they were in awe of the masculinity gliding across the room like a panther. Her eyes couldn't help but be drawn to his ass, and it looked especially fine under those leathers, not to mention the more-than-obvious bulge in the front of them. The room started to get spotty, and Laura realized she'd been holding her breath. *What the fuck?* was all she could get to run through her mind.

"Well! Guess by the look on your face that you approve of our newest service Dom!" Steve walked up to the bar and took a stool. Even in the dim lighting, Steve could see Laura's face turn three shades of red.

"Cabrizzi? Are you kidding?" she asked, incredulous. "You can't be serious!"

"Look at him, Laura. Tell me you don't want that," Steve grinned.

"No. I don't." *Do I?*

"Liar. Have a fun evening. I'll check on you in a bit." Steve walked away and left Laura to stew.

"Hey, can I get a diet soda?" Vic asked as he leaned backward against the bar. Laura hadn't seen him come up, and she jumped about a foot. "Damn, woman, I just want a drink. I'm not gonna slap you or anything. Calm down," he snapped, not even cracking a smile.

"Don't you want your usual beer?" she asked, surprised that he'd asked for a soft drink.

"Nope. Against the rules."

"Whose rules?" Laura asked.

"Mine." She sat the drink in front of him and he picked up the glass. She couldn't help but notice how elegant his hands were, long, strong fingers with just the lightest dusting of dark hair across them. Looking at them made her feel odd. "Can't drink alcohol and keep my wits about me with a sub."

"You're serious about this, aren't you?" Laura asked, her mouth hanging open.

The new Vic Cabrizzi looked into her eyes and asked, "And what would make you think I'm not?" The low growl in his voice made her insides quiver, and she had to look away. "That's exactly what I thought." He finished the drink and smacked the glass onto the bar, then walked away. *What the hell?*, Laura thought. She looked down at her hands – they were visibly shaking.

Several of the unattached women in the club spent most of the evening talking to Vic, but most of them wanted to be collared by a Dom – right that minute. And Vic was not interested in that at all. They could flirt all they wanted, but it got them nowhere. He made it clear: He was a service Dom, and he'd be glad to meet their needs, but that was it.

"Oh my god! He's so gorgeous!" one woman was gushing as she and another woman walked up to the bar. "Can I have a Bud Light?" she asked Laura, who pulled it and sat it down in front of her.

"I'd take him on in a New York minute," her friend said. "I needed a sign that said 'slippery when wet' just standing there talking to him!" Laura wanted to hurl.

"I want to climb up there and let him spank me good, but he's so damn big, he's kinda scary," the first one said. *Ha! Wish he could hear that!*, Laura thought.

But that left her wondering why she wanted him to fail. He'd obviously worked hard to train with Alex. She should be happy for him, that he was more confident and looked better, happier, than she'd ever seen him. Why did seeing him looking and feeling good make her feel so bad? *Maybe I'm the bitch that José said I am.*

Laura felt her phone vibrate in her pocket and she pulled it out to see an unfamiliar number on the screen.

She'd advertised to try to find a roommate, and she hoped that someone was responding. When she answered the call, a male voice said something, but the club was too loud. "Hang on just a minute, please. I can't hear you." She looked around – no Steve. "Hey, Vic!" she yelled. Vic broke away from a beautiful, bare-breasted brunette and came over to the bar. "Hey, I've got a phone call. Can you watch the bar for just a minute?"

"Yeah, but just a minute. Get your ass right on back here," he said. He'd never talked to her like that before, and she was taken aback, but she didn't have time to worry about that.

Jetting out the side door behind the bar, she put the phone back up to her ear. "Yeah, sorry about that. Can I help you? Are you calling about the ad for a roommate."

"No." Something about the voice made her feel odd. "Laura? Laura Billings?" Her hands went cold and a buzzing started in her ears. "Billings?"

"Who the hell is this?" she growled into the phone.

"Laura, I'm so sorry to call you and drag all of this up. This is Brewster. Please don't hang up on me."

"DON'T CALL ME AGAIN!" Laura screamed into the phone, then hit END and dropped the phone on the ground. It promptly rang again; same number.

She stared at the phone. Everything was coming at her in a rush, and the earth seemed to tilt. She hit ACCEPT and asked through gritted teeth, "What the hell do you want?"

"Laura, please, don't hang up. I need to talk to you. I want to make this right; we all do. Well, almost all of us. I hear a lot of noise in the background. Can I call you later? Or tomorrow? It's important."

"I can't believe you'd have the nerve to call me. How did you find me?" she was whispering, feeling so weak that she could barely speak.

"Billings, I know it's hard to believe, but I want to make this right. It's eaten at me for years, ruined my life and I'm betting yours too, and it's time to man up. Please. Let me do this, me and the others. Please?"

Laura's head was spinning and she felt like she was going to throw up. It was a little late for an apology, but it was more than she'd gotten over the last sixteen years, sixteen years of sheer hell. "Call me tomorrow. Ten o'clock tomorrow morning. That's Eastern Time."

"Okay. Ten o'clock tomorrow morning. Will do." The phone went dead. Laura stood staring at the phone, her hands trembling so violently that she could barely hold it. After a minute or two, she walked back through the side door and up to the bar.

"Where the hell were you?" Vic barked. Then he got a good look at her face. "God, Laura, what's wrong?" She stared at the bar, and Vic grabbed her arms and spun her to look at him. "Talk to me. What is it?"

Laura shook his hands off. "Don't touch me. Leave me alone. Nothing's wrong." She grabbed the towel and started wiping.

She heard Vic say, "That's a lie. I don't believe it for a minute. And when you decide you need someone to talk to about whatever just happened, find me. I can't speak for anyone else, but you can always trust me. I'd never hurt you, not in a million years." Laura turned to apologize to him for the way she'd talked to him, but he was gone.

Vic walked into the men's locker room and leaned against the wall. He knew damn well something had happened, but the ice princess wasn't going to tell him what or take any help from anyone. And he was done with trying to get someone who didn't want to be around him to open up to him. That was a dead-end street, and he'd walked down too many of them already.

From Renovating a Heart, Book 3 in the **Love Under Construction Series**

An hour and fifteen minutes into his Wednesday work day, his phone buzzed. "Steve, your nine thirty appointment is here."

"Yeah, okay, it's . . ."

"Miss Markham?"

Steve wracked his brain – he didn't know a woman named Markham. "Send her on in." He put his jacket and his professional face on, then took his seat behind the big mahogany desk.

The door opened and Angela, Steve's assistant, ushered the woman in. Steve's eyes went wide and a huge smile spread across his face. "Kelly!"

"Hi Steve! Wow, nice office!"

"Thanks! I didn't recognize your last name. Glad to see you! Want something to drink?" She shook her head. "So what can I do for you?" he asked, motioning for her to sit in one of the chairs in front of his desk.

Pinkness spread across her cheeks and her hands shook as she pulled a document out of her purse. "I talked to Nikki. She said you were the person I needed to talk to; she said you'd understand." Steve unfolded the document she passed to him.

It was a submissive's contract. He blinked a couple of times to be certain he was seeing it correctly. Sure enough, the submissive's name was plain on the top of the document: Kelly Markham. Now he understood why Nikki had sent her to him. "This was very well done. Did he break the contract with you?"

"Sort of." Kelly's gaze fell to her hands in her lap. "He passed."

"Oh my god! I'm so sorry! How long ago was this?"

"Nine years." She sniffed. "I still miss him every day."

Steve came around from his desk chair to the armchair next to Kelly. "So how can I help?"

"He made this out thinking it would protect me. Then when he died and we weren't married, his kids took everything, even some of the gifts he'd given me over the years. I'm about the same age as they are, so they saw me as a gold-digger who just wanted him for his money. They even called me a pervert because they didn't understand our lifestyle. I would've married him if he'd ever asked, but he never did. But he loved me, he really did, and I loved him. Even though I could've used the money, I just gave up – it wasn't about money to start with. And I've done okay until Friday when I lost my job. We think they want to close the branch of the insurance company where I worked, and they just laid me off. I've got three months' severance and I'll draw unemployment, but it's not much. I know Dom/sub contracts aren't legally binding, but I was wondering if . . ."

"No, they're not. But this one clearly shows intent. He genuinely thought he'd protected you by making this contract. I wish it had worked." Steve thought for a minute. "You know, I don't want to get your hopes up, but let me see if I can find something, a case precedent or a loophole, anything, that could help. Can I make a copy of this?"

"Sure! Please! How much will you charge me? Because I don't have any . . ."

"You're Nikki's friend, and you took Laura in when she needed a place to hide. Just consider this my way of repaying you."

"Oh, no, I couldn't . . ."

"Oh yes, you can and you will." Steve took the contract out to Angela and asked her to make him a copy. When he came back, he asked Kelly, "Did Nikki by any chance tell you . . ."

"That you're in the lifestyle? Yeah. That's why she told me to come and talk to you."

"Did she tell you that I have a fetish club in Lexington?" *Boy, I'd love to see her in nothing but a smile!*, he thought.

"No! She didn't! I'd love to visit sometime." Kelly's eyes were sparkling now.

"I'd love for you to visit. We'll be open tomorrow night. If you'd like to come by, I'll show you around."

"I'll do that. And thanks, Steve. I really appreciate this."

"No problem." As she left, he handed her a card for the club with his signature on the back. He was glad she'd come in, and he hoped she'd come by and like the club enough to stick around, because he was itching to see those tits bare. He knew they were fake, but they were real enough for him.

I hope you enjoyed these excerpts from the* Love Under Construction *series. Check your favorite online retailer for the format that works best with your electronic device.

Connect with Deanndra on Substance B

Substance B is a new platform for independent authors to directly connect with their readers. Please visit Deanndra's Substance B page where you can:

- Sign up for Deanndra's newsletter
- Send a message to Deanndra
- See all platforms where Deanndra's books are sold
- Request autographed eBooks from Deanndra

Visit Substance B today to learn more about your favorite independent authors.

CPSIA information can be obtained
at www.ICGtesting.com
Printed in the USA
FSOW02n2045060117
29354FS